What Fear Was

What Fear Was

Ben Walter

PUNCHER & WATTMANN

First published in 2022
Published by Puncher and Wattmann
PO Box 279
Waratah NSW 2298
http://www.puncherandwattmann.com
puncherandwattmann@bigpond.com

ISBN 9781922571205

Cover design by Miranda Douglas
Text design and typesetting by Morgan Arnett
Printed by Lightning Source

Cover image:

Troy Ruffels
The bone gardens, 2017
Digital print on composite aluminium sheet
220 x 330 cm
Edition of 12 + 1 AP

© Troy Ruffels 2017

Courtesy of the Artist and Bett Gallery Hobart
https://www.bettgallery.com.au

A catalogue record for this book is available from the National Library of Australia

For Rachel.

Contents

Flathead Out One Day   9

The Economist   17

The Lake   21

Wrapped in Ice, Speaking   29

Conglomerate   35

We Are All Superman   57

It's All Happening Here   59

Landscape within Landscapes   63

The Eradication Program   69

All Hollows   79

The Slide   85

Atlantis Minor   93

Below Tree Level   99

Beast Evolving   111

Surely You Can't Be Serious   115

A Visitor's Guide to the Huts of Mount Wellington: 1913   121

Be My Dora   133

What Fear Was   139

Here Are the Holes in My Eyes   143

The Day the Music Died   151

An Anti-Glacier Book   157

The Bridge   165

Acknowledgements   173

Flathead Out One Day

When you step into the grey boat it bows to the applauding waves and nods to those retreating then it settles on its stage, poised to break into another round of curtain calls as the wind from the south hurls petals of spray. There are clouds flexing high and grinding so much sleet out of the air – it sparks against your face and tries to fill the boat like a great bowl of water to be drunk by the ever-thirsty sea.

Your mother is wasting in her bed. Her skin is a poor, bedraggled blanket covering her body and her moans are the wind; they carry across the water as you bolt your feet to the centre of the deck, and even though the sleet is freezing your red flannel shirt to your back and the wind is tearing at its buttons, you find a certain stillness in all that storm.

For she thought she could manage to eat one fish. And there are five sleek flathead lined up on parade against the boat's deck, their olive green skin covered with shining scales, spiked fins standing to attention.

'Where are we?' asks one flathead. 'Our mother is calling us.'

They blink up at you in the burning air.

'Boat,' you tell them straight. 'You're on a boat.'

The flathead whimper and one of them begins to sing a mournful song about swimming across the underwater meadows, huddling in the sand's corrugations and biting at fingernail crabs. The others join in. Listening to their chorus, you remember your own mother watching with care and concern as you played in the yard with your brother, the old swing surging. Pity flecks your thought; one by one, you pinch the jaws of four fish, their small teeth pressing into your skin, and flick them back into the sea.

The remaining fish looks at you with steady eyes.

You are feeling very hungry.

'When you do it,' he asks, 'can you fillet my flesh?'

You slice your knife behind his fin, cutting away at the meat clinging to his backbone, and you swallow those fillets and bury what remains of his body in the waves.

When you ease back on to the jetty, everything is still.

You walk along the boards and step down into a second boat. It is a wooden clinker dinghy, tied up on the other side. There are no fish there.

You return to the first boat, but it has disappeared.

You walk back to the second boat and climb in.

The wind is easing and easting and the sleet has softened into light moths of fluttering snow. Now, there are four flathead waiting on the deck, shifting their stiff tails and bodies into crescents and arcs.

One of them looks up at you. 'We're on a boat, aren't we?' she says. 'I'm sure we're on a boat.'

'Well,' you say. 'It certainly *looks* like you're on a boat.'

'We're on a boat,' she says again, and the four flathead begin to cry. Small salty tears seep from their eyes and pool on their splayed faces, and she explains that they can hear their mother calling from over the hills of swell, a desperate cry that carries like the song of whales; they want to leap into the water, back into the comfort of her broad body, and you think of sleeping by your own mother on the torn brown couch, worn out by grief. You feel troubled by these fish; but also, still, a little hungry.

As you tip three of them back into the ocean, you are sure there is something you are forgetting.

The remaining fish stares at you with deep holes in her eyes.

'Gut me,' she says. 'Rip out my guts and toss them to the gulls and pick around my bones for any flesh you want.'

You slit open her skin and tear out her stomach and her heart. The juices and blood slick over your fingers as you throw her innards over your shoulder, then you nibble at her flesh and feel its soft wetness slide down your throat.

You get out of the clinker dinghy and walk back along the silent jetty. The first boat is back. There is a small anchor sitting in the bow.

A seagull stands on a rotting post nearby. You watch him for a moment, then turn back to the boat.

The anchor is gone and a chain leads down into the water. You walk slowly down the jetty to the second boat. It is filled with a thousand fish in a flapping heap. Whiting, shark, gurnard, couta and trevally – the gunwales are nearly taking on water.

You turn back to see that the first boat has disappeared, but there is another boat sitting just behind where it had been berthed, a yellow fibreglass runabout with glistening lines. The song of the flathead echoes in your ears and you spin around as though footsteps are knocking on the jetty's planks. The song drifts out to sea and you notice that the clinker dinghy is empty now; it still smells strongly of fish.

You stride up the jetty and climb aboard the third boat. The wind has petered out its breath and the temperature is stretching into mild warmth. You pretend not to notice three flathead lying on the deck. One of them tries to catch your attention. 'Hello,' he says, waving a fin. 'Hey, hello?'

'Oh,' you say. 'Sorry, I didn't see you there.'

'What the hell are we doing in this boat?' he asks.

'Boat?' you say. 'I'm not sure this is a boat, I think it is … oh no, you're right, it does seem we're on some sort of boat.'

'Jeez, we shouldn't be on a boat,' says the flathead, coughing and groaning. 'Our mother says that boats are just shit.'

'Well, I don't know,' you reply. 'My brother used to love boats.'

But the fish beats through your uncertainty; he explains that they are sick, that there are lice burrowing into their skin and bleeding in their gums, and they can hear their mother calling from a small cave where they know they will be cared for and nursed back to health, and you remember stories of your own mother holding you in the night as you coughed and spluttered with drowning lungs, desperate not to lose another son; how your home was dark, even as the windows were clear, bright eyes that waited for you to recover, the whole house waiting for the fever to drop, hands in its lap, marking time in its tired old seat for the hours to pass into days – the whole house tense and stressed, for there was nothing, absolutely nothing it could do; loved ones walking from room to room and all the rooms so dark.

For some reason you no longer feel hungry. You nudge two of the fish back into the water with your boot.

The remaining flathead looks at you. 'When you eat me, eat me whole.'

You hear the faint cry of your mother sobbing across the flattened sea, then you swallow that fish in one great slurp with all its scales and slime. It scratches and slides and spikes down your throat, and then the fish is swimming in your gut and your stomach churns like a dead pool draining. You jump in a hurry from the yellow runabout like you are seasick, even in the flattening swell.

Where are the first two boats? There is a large ferry blocking the view. Busy fish are embarking in thousands of fluttering queues. You stroll up to the entryway and there is a bullshark with his broad chest and whippy tail.

You do not have a ticket.

You try to shuffle aboard with your legs bound together, arms angled from your sides like spindly fins, but the bullshark blocks your way. The lean light glints on his silver fins and his snout looks stern. His eyes are wide and teeth peer from his gums.

You back away, pat your pockets, look around for a ticket booth.

It is hard to tell on the jetty whether it is day or night.

'Too late,' says the shark. 'Fuck off.' And he grins at you maliciously. 'Don't forget your mother,' he says. 'Aren't you forgetting your mother?'

He laughs as he closes a netted gate at the end of the gangway.

As the ferry begins to float away from the jetty, you run towards it, but all too quickly it is five, ten metres away. Skidding on old scales, you nearly slip off the edge into deep water; breathing great gusts, you bend at the raised edge of the jetty and form a fist, rasping your knuckles against the wood as the ferry slips away and the bullshark snorts across the waves.

When you turn back to the jetty all three of the boats have returned; they have been joined by a fourth. As you walk back with watchful steps the other dinghies blur and fade and it is just the fourth boat waiting there, a small purdon with peeling white paint, barely ten feet long with a tiny outboard motor perched on the stern like a mosquito.

You get into the fourth dinghy.

There are two flathead sitting on the deck. One is wearing a shirt and jeans, the other a light dress. They seem to have been whispering among themselves, but they trickle into silence when you get in beside them.

'Hi,' you say.

The fish look at each other.

'What's going on?' you ask.

'Nothing,' say the flathead.

'Sorry,' you say. 'I didn't mean to interrupt. This looked like a nice bar. My throat feels kind of dry, so I figured I'd stop for a drink.'

'This isn't a bar,' says one of the flathead. 'This is a boat.'

'What do you mean, a boat?' you reply. 'This is a bar.'

A phone rings. *I have to take this,* mouths one of the flathead. He answers the phone. 'Mum?' he says. 'Yes, Mum, I know it's late. It's okay, my sister's here, we'll be fine. We'll be careful.'

'Hey, I'm talking to you,' you say.

'Huh … that's nobody, Mum,' says the fish.

'Nobody?' you say. 'Listen, cunt, hang up.'

The fish start to look nervous.

'Right now,' you insist.

'Mum,' says the flathead, 'I gotta go.' He hangs up and looks up at you. 'Come on man, do we have to do this?'

And even though your stomach is full, even though you are no longer hungry, you crack your knuckles and stretch out your shoulders.

'It's all for my mother,' you say.

'Don't you mean your brother?' asks the flathead.

You are suddenly confused.

This makes you even angrier.

The flathead looks resigned.

'Make it quick,' he says, 'and please don't hurt my sister.'

The weather is warm and the sun is shining bright.

You shove the flathead's sister out of the way, fingernails scratching at her scales as she scampers into the water, and you grab the flathead and bash his head against the side of the boat and then you leave him on the deck for flies to strike hard.

As you get out of the dinghy you are breathing heavily and the sickness in your gut is becoming overwhelming.

There are dinghies of every colour down both sides of the jetty.

They are all empty.

You close your eyes, open them.

They are still there, but now they are filled with life jackets.

You pace slowly down the jetty, looking from side to side as though you are searching for the right address on a scrubby street. You feel a shadow behind you, a deep shadow, as though a large grey naval ship with a skate standing at a gun has eased into harbour and is lining up its sights. Panicked, you start running for the shoreline. You hear a clicking, a scratching. You're not going to make it.

You jump into one of the dinghies at random.

It looks like your brother's dinghy.

The life jackets are gone.

This is not a safe boat.

You've got to get out of there.

Trembling, you leap back on to the jetty.

Now, it is the only boat. The warship has motored off or sunk; but with its shadow lost, the sun is blinding hot and the jetty is searing your feet. You are choking on the dry air and blades of sunlight are slashing into your flesh. You can't bring yourself to risk hiding in your brother's dinghy, so you leap into the open water.

For a moment you hang in the air, listening to your mother gasping across the waves, and you remember – and then the deep drags you down and there is another longing cry beneath the surface, reverberating in your skin and down your throat, calling to your bones and your muscles, your heart and guts.

Beside you lies one last flathead with his ears cocked.

He waits as you cower in the sand at the bottom of the sea.

The Economist

They are clouds or they are leaves. They hang in bunches over my head and the leaves rain down and the grass is green and wet with them. They are dark and their gloom is like a fish that has swum its life staring at the water and at nothing. 'Kick,' you might have told me, 'kick kick kick,' but there is oil in the water, there is so much silt that the water is groaning with the load and every droplet is painted the same shade of mud.

I have been without any work for a long time and the listless days are heavy for being so bare: days when I've carved no steps into the story's pages, days when I've annotated no clocks, written no words above the straight lines of minute hands and hours.

For two years I have been applying for jobs, contemptuous jobs that purse up their lips and turn sharply from my pleas, jobs that fold up their arms, stare me down and send me back to the slums of disappointment and misery with a slowly stretching finger, pointing me along the chipped road to my overgrown underground flat with its dirt-brown carpet and dirt-dirt walls. If these jobs had feet and their feet had boots they would stamp me down in the dust. If these jobs had hearts they would reach down with their hands (if these jobs had hands) and they would pick me up and hold me, stroke my soft and wilting hair as they told me that it simply couldn't be, but that they felt for me – oh how they felt for me – but they just couldn't, and you just couldn't, and the bedclothes were cold, they were always so cold.

These are not just any jobs; they are starlets and celebrities that put on a dance number in the middle of a street with its cars all agape and its jaws dropping down along the pavement in the domino breeze. Striding in unpatched jeans, I bypass the window offers in cafes and bars, the newspaper columns seeking chefs, managers and qualified precision. I have set my sights higher and I am certain that the odds will play out in time. For I am only applying for jobs that have been advertised in *The Economist*.

This week I applied for the Director (Budget) in the Division of Financial Management at UNICEF. I'm determined to make something of myself, for then you would see my photograph in serious weekly papers and note that I am a man who can weigh and calculate important matters, a man who others look to for guidance and judgement. You would knock on my door and fling me open and we would cry till the day was pencilled in evening shades, until finally I would be dragged away by the very tip of my immaculate tie to meetings in twelve-star hotels and champagne glasses and ballistic missiles, and you would be there applauding me as though I were walking on stage to receive a prize.

But – and it is late at night, the darkness has brought us a little closer, for who can say whether or not you are sitting across from me in this deep ocean of evening – there is one small thing that I fear. Do you know what it is? I fear that one Friday morning, as a small wave of wakefulness flushes me from my bed and I shuffle into my kitchenette to coax the kettle's poor spirits, I will slump down with my phone at the Nullarbor bench where I'll thumb through my emails, and there amid the messages that I have read and not read and left to prick at my administrative conscience, there will be one that seems a little more embossed or bordered in gold, and this message will proudly proclaim that I've been chosen to be the director of a major financial or perhaps environmental institution; that they'll ship me off to Paris or Brussels where they will measure my arms and legs for that suit and tie, and they'll hand me a leather brown briefcase holding many papers in cream yellow folders and an electronic device that fits into my ear. I will sit down in my office and pick up the phone, and all day, all week and all year that phone will usher in subordinates who will ask me what we are going to do with that forest and this village and that mango and this child's face, until one night I will look at my watch and it will be time to hang up and I will hurry out to my limousine which is the full length of a city block, and I'll be carried off to another ancient city of gleaming steel. I'll be escorted to the most prominent of those crystalline buildings and carried up to the highest peak of its floors, where I will meet other people in positions of power and prestige, and 'Bill,' one will be saying, 'I'm so glad to meet you' (and this will be the director of a hedge fund the size of Malaysia's economy) and for the briefest of moments I will look at all those pillars of people who have been built from the city and are part of the city and are holding the city together, and I will feel like a thin and insubstantial interloper sidling in to steal the sea-blue cheeses. 'You know,' I will say, fiddling with the twig stem of my glass, 'Harry, it's really good to meet you too, but I have to admit that I kind of wonder...just last week I was sitting in my Moonah flat with its tyres stolen and the windscreen cracked, ironing my one good shirt and watching *A Current Affair,* and now here I am, making these decisions that change the very angles of the earth. Doesn't it feel that something doesn't quite add up?'

And perhaps the chandeliers will be scattering honesty through the room in a thousand fillets of light, for Harry will reach a finger to his throat and adjust his collar as though it is part of a costume or shell, and he will look from side to side at all the bustling eminence and then he will lean in towards me. 'You know,' he'll whisper, 'We're all like you. We're all exactly the same. Don't worry about any of that.'

And this is what I fear: as I shake his trembling hand and then sidle over to look through the vast window at the city hurtling with glowing clouds, I will look for you among all the lights that hurry around me, and I won't be able to see your face at all.

The Lake

For Manny

It's then that I lose heart. My mind trickles to a stop at the bottom of a hill; while staring at nothing at all on the ground with downcast half-eyes, I watch the small aeroplane turn on its heel and stroll across the field, drawing momentum up through blades of shaved grass. Tiny faces in the windows, dirty white paint. Dad is at my side speaking steadily, hopefully, insistently. The six-seater clenches itself and springs.

'We can walk,' says Dad. 'We were going to walk.' His arm, slung across my shoulders, is a block of wood. There are layers separating our flesh; we are insulated from each other's touch. In the edges of black peppermints, rosellas can be heard above the engine noise, rosellas or goshawks, currawongs or some other primal form of the stretch towards flying that has caved in my head, as though I had stumbled under the small plane's propellers, jumped from its soaring curves.

There is yes, there is no. There is wander back to the car or remain here, longing uselessly towards the barren strip. These are channels without water. Dad's fingers press into the swells of my shoulder like he is operating machinery, as if we are already back in the car hurtling between the verges of rough grass, parading ferns and loping hills blacking out the view.

It has been a frenzy of driving; lining the roads with our cramping tyres, gear changes under strict orders. The greasy wrappers bunched at our feet with the tent, clothes and sleeping bags slumped in the back like bored children. 'Dad,' I would shout. 'Turn off! I've never been to Tunbridge. I want to reach into the sandstone, I want to work the old mill and flake flour down my jeans.' His gaze pressing against the black highway. He has been driving alone and I have been the radio blending with his trance.

He has always been this way. Weeks of bushwalking through summer were hobbled by his race against days. Every ribbon that indicated the track was a finish line to tear past as the buttongrass cheered in the wind. The knee-deep mud, roots snaking our boots, a steeplechase obstructing our undulating way. No time to linger easily at a rivulet or fallen tree, to appreciate the hasty view of New River Lagoon; brisk, flickering images of wind-struck water and fluttering oars that could never settle into watercolours. Millie traipsing along with her sleeping bag snailed on her back, Dad trudging with a Sherpa's pack mountaineering over his head.

One year we used the inheritance from his father's heart attack to plunge into Europe. 'Michael,' Mum had suggested, 'can't we just take the trains?' He had plotted the schedules and agreed. We blurred on high-speed rail from Paris to Rome; a day of cannonballing through colonnades, dragged left and right, over bridges and under catacombs and then on to the next seat of government with its check-list of crumbling splendour.

As I grew older and felt every journey's experiences lurching away like the evening pademelons toying with our car, I dug deeper tones in my voice. Sitting shoulder to shoulder on frustrated day trips to waypoints, I would yell at him: 'Stop the car. Now. It's dark, the last campsite's coming up, quit being such a stubborn old bastard and stop the bloody car.'

Every couple of days he might be persuaded to enjoy a uranium mine, a horseshoed waterfall, a jagged bridge; not frequently enough to continue travelling with him. It has been years since we have gone anywhere together, and while he has greyed and diminished, it's only to refine himself into a keener and more determined certainty. A father-and-son trip, he suggested.

I still don't know how we agreed to pack up for Easter and join the thin, intent hordes streaming out to see the impoundment that was losing itself in a tiny, simple lake. For only the fourth time in a hundred years it was draining, letting its flood go. The rotting, saturated vegetation, the wet stench. Dead poles rising from the ground, old worms re-emerging and breathing.

Everybody wondered as they packed up their cars. Was it energy demands? Had we been so busy playing with our electric hands, a slow drain pouring power across our towns and drying out the dams? Or wider climatic factors, the Spanish kids messing round with water fights on the beach? The distant butterflies and carbon and orbits? Every few years the reservoir would drop a metre or two, maybe even more on a rare, parched decade, but an absolute drain back to the lake was out of the box.

Bream, perch and galaxias, dying flags flapping on the ground. Confused pelicans, sandpipers and honeyeaters packing up and heading to more watery turf. The beach, the long, pink beach eyebrowed across the lake's eastern end, glistening in the new sun.

I would have walked in myself, made my pilgrimage on aching feet squelching through the mess of soggy bottom, scouring out the track. But he was determined that we go together. He wanted it marked, this occasion, like a painting left in a will. Early on the first day, as we wolfed burgers scavenged from a chained drive-through joint, it was clear that we were continuing our regular service, striving with speed limits, frustration and resentment.

Initially, the aeroplane was a pretext for further antagonism. Through tedious kilometres we scanned the advertising signs boarding the faces of general stores, then shared a discussion late the second night. An older bloke on his way back home took an interest. 'What you really want to be doing is going up in one of those little beauties. Different perspective, mate, nothing like it really, and you pass right over all of that stink.' The next morning, as we drove past yet another historical turnoff, I told him that I wanted to take a flight. For once, speeding down the highway, he looked across at me. 'A flight, what do you mean a flight? We're walking. We'll see the thing on our own feet. Don't need carrying.'

'We're flying,' I repeated. 'I've never done that. Come all this way. Might as well, it's what you're supposed to do. Be like the picture, framed over the fire.'

The forest thinned out to high moorland; a few cattle loped quietly. The windscreen speckled with whisperings of drizzle. 'You flew in to Melaleuca when we walked the south coast,' he offered, a few minutes later.

'It wasn't to see,' I said. 'I want to just see. We can walk as well, what's it going to take? An extra couple of hours? C'mon, it's something different.'

It was becoming something I really wanted to do, substituting for all the lost opportunities to witness something unique; an expensive, vicarious extravagance.

Dad flicked on the wipers and watched them scrape across the glass, collecting rare drops. 'No flight, we're walking,' he pronounced in solidarity with the boots standing at attention in the back of the car, the day packs, jackets and scroggin.

But I didn't let up through our third day of driving. 'We'll still walk, I just want to do the plane. I'll pay.' A frown trenched across his warzone face. 'Listen, you stupid old man, we're going to take the bloody plane.' Staring grimly forwards, fists on the wheel, at my throat. At half-past six, the sun about to set and the darkness drifting in, he finally conceded dinner at Strathgordon, fried batter embracing limp hints of cabbage and beef. Afterwards, wiping oily hands on my trousers, I refused to get back in the car.

'If you're not willing to take the plane tomorrow I'm not going any further. Go on yourself and see the lake, I don't care anymore. Go on, hurry up, there's a pub here with rooms, that'll do me tonight, I'll meet you on the way out tomorrow night. Bugger off.'

He stood there, handling the door. Thoughtfully opened it wide and got in. Started the car. One elbow leaning on the window, arm bending back to press his fist against his temple. Other hand on the wheel. Eyes focused directly through the windscreen. He grabbed the gear-stick, changed into first, revved the engine while riding the clutch and then eased back, rolling forward a few centimetres. Stopped. He sighed broadly and turned to look at me. 'All right, we'll do the bloody flight. Now get in the car, we need to move.'

'Where?' I asked carefully, walking slowly to my door. 'How much further we going to go? Not going to camp on the airfield are we?'

'Don't argue,' he said, 'just get in.' He sounded more tired than angry, as though three days of driving had finally caught up with him. 'There's a campsite about fifteen minutes on, we'll do that yes? Then on to the plane in the morning.'

A subdued night, the motions of ripping out and setting the tent and turning in early.

I was up with the first colour to find him sipping at tea from his burning enamel cup, nodding towards me. 'Nice day for it.' I sat down by the cool fuel stove and checked the stained water under the lid. 'Should be right,' he said. 'Strong, but just brewed a few minutes back.' I fetched a cup, washed it out roughly and drank.

There were clouds in the sky, a little wind. We packed up the tent, damp with dew, and draped it in the rear of the station wagon. Stretched out our shoulders and our necks, then fell once more into the cloth seats that were moulding themselves around our worn bodies.

'Mate,' says the bloke at the rough caravan serving as a booking desk outside the agricultural airstrip, 'we'd love to take you, but you gotta get in line. We're booked solid for like a month. Got people calling and emailing from the US, China.'

'Made a special trip,' says Dad gruffly, fingering his wallet. 'Can't make an exception for locals? Not got special flights or nothing?'

The man shakes his head. 'She's just a little plane, mate, no seven-whatever-seven, and they're bussing them in now on tours. If we had a cancellation could let you know, got coverage out here have you? Still be days though, we've got a waiting list camping over by the creek. People come and they go, but they make sure their names are on the list. Got it here somewhere.' He rummages around in a mess of papers spilling from a desk, to the floor, towards the bin. 'Yep. You'd be twenty-four and five.'

'Can't do anything for us then?' asks Dad.

I shake my head and say quietly, 'Look, we're buggered, let's just go.'

'Nothing at all?' Dad asks again. He winks, forces a smile and tilts his head towards me. 'The old man was at the picket on the river, back when. Boy just wants to see it all from up there.'

'Love to help you,' the bloke says, leaning against the caravan's window sill. He tries to look sympathetic. 'Be better off going back to town. They got operators working from there, shorter trips of course but you'd see it, wouldn't you? That's what you want. Don't remember how long it goes, just as long as you get to see it.'

I walk away from their motions of negotiation and stare across the field as the latest group cluster themselves into the plane. The pilot helps the last passenger into the cab, an old man done up in travelling polo and chinos, wide-eyed camera peering from his chest. Talks them through what must be safety instructions. Dad is beginning to remonstrate, but I am drifting, flowing out of myself; my hands are on my hips and I am looking down. I watch as the engine starts and the plane begins to amble through the field. The noise is boastful, pathetic. My palms are cased in fists and there are wires in my neck. I am leaning down and staring at the toes of my boots, scuffed with paint, collisions with dirt and rock, trailing strips of rubber from their soles.

Dad has walked deliberately across and put a hairy arm across my back. 'What do you reckon,' he says.

'Don't know,' I say quietly, 'don't know.'

'We'll walk it,' he says, 'we were always going to walk it.'

'Don't know,' I say again, feeling light tears coating my eyes. I know that I need to sleep or to eat; it's the exhaustion, the blood sugar, the constant driving and the conflict. It's all of these things and it's losing sight of the forbidden plane as it specks the sky, speeds towards the old lake that is briefly resuming its past. How long before it will be covered in a fog of fresh water?

He grabs my arm and leads me over to the gravel road, one step after another.

'C'mon,' he says. 'We've got to keep going. Get in the car. Get back in the car, mate.'

Wrapped in Ice, Speaking

You are drowning in riptide snow on a hazardous peak in the Uttarakhand region of India with your friends. It is so much tougher than anything you have ever climbed before, a monstrous wolf of a peak with its ears pricked up, and you are haunted by strong and persuasive longings to tuck yourself into the beds around you and pull up the sheets for ever, lying there with the frozen bodies buried in the air and the wind. You struggle to the top, tiptoe the peak's summit and hug your companions – the warmth of their bodies is distant, hidden behind so many layers – but the mountain has noticed you. On the way down, heavy with the burden of numb and clumsy limbs, Lisa slips down an icy cliff and breaks her leg. The fractured bone is not as white as the ice, but you feel a whole lot colder.

'Oh, fucking shit,' she yells as the tears are ripped from her eyes.

Her husband fumbles in his pack for the first aid kit; rolls a bandage around the bone, splints her leg as best he can. A desperate calm soaks your body as you help drag her into the lee of the wind.

'It's going to be fine,' you repeat as you ease her on to the emergency sled, hands cupping her shoulders. Strands of hair slip from her hood and tangle your fingers. 'It's going to be fine.'

It feels like a benediction or kaddish.

~

On the long ridges it seems that you might make it. Guiding the sled in slow steps down; a long breath exhaled. Easy running on gentle slopes, correcting the sled from front and back. You sink to the valley like a feather in an ocean.

But then you come across the first body, a woman in black and red gear with her face all gone and her fingers there, resting her head on a grey forgiving rock, the snow creeping around her torso in a light embrace. As you skirt her on the left, assessing the edge, she pushes herself out of the ice.

'I'm sorry,' she mumbles. 'I'm terribly sorry.'

She lifts a chapped hand, trying to point, and there is another huge cliff, so many metres of vertical spite that snatch at the time you have left as you rig the ropes and ease Lisa down, her body getting colder and her face all locked, and you wonder if Dom is thinking of when you were all younger and shooting for peaks, the time he was wheezing and coughing and his skin was reflecting the sky. 'Edema,' Lisa's sharp eyes had noted. 'Dom, it's pulmonary edema, we've got to get you down.' Through all his feeble protests and the planning you had put in to the trip, through all of that stubborn momentum, you gave up early and saved his life.

And now it is his turn and he is stuffing it up by going too slow. The night is catching up and he has started using your words – 'it's going to be fine, it's going to be fine' – and you are certain he feels troubled by this repetition; that somehow, your reassurance is more authentic and he is just an echo, thin tones pulsing off the cliffs. Lisa is silent, wrapped up in herself. The night trips you up and punches you in the guts and the wind blows you over and the snow is just fucking with you for fun and you reach the top of the worst descent, a nightmare of thirty metres and multiple pitches and probably tarantulas and tigers, and there at the top is the second body, a bleached green back with his head buried in scree, an ice axe gripped in one hand and clothes all dangling from his body in spiderwebbed rags. His voice comes murmuring through the trembling rocks.

'You've had it,' he says. 'You're fucked.'

Somehow, Lisa chips her way out of her fugue. 'He's right,' she says. 'Leave me.'

It's like a curse: words that can never be taken back. Your heart trembles; you want to look at Lisa, stroke her pale skin.

Dom tries to protest but his lips are wood.

'We'll give it a go,' he tries to argue, 'there's still time.'

'We talked about this,' she gasps.

Her husband turns away and prepares the ropes.

'Talked about it,' she repeats.

Dom keeps at the ropes but they have fallen down, they are lying on the snow and his gloved fingers are twisting and knotting around each other.

You are standing back as though this is a small domestic disturbance over the proper method of grilling fish.

Dom reaches for his wife and kisses her. He cries ice tears as she fades, and then you leave her there on the sled and begin to pick your way down the rock face.

~

In the morning the tent is a shell; your arms and legs are filled with stones. You barely made it down the cliff. The frost had crept into your fingers and toes, it had danced on your faces and snuck into your souls; about two-thirds of the way down the escarpment you had climbed past the third body, hanging from a line hammered into the rock and draped in a Canadian flag.

'You're next,' he said. A camera was poking out from the red and white shroud and as the body swung there, it took a picture of your defeated faces.

You managed to note it was windy and dark.

The photo would be blurred.

Suck shit.

You had mostly fallen down the last pitch before tumbling into the half-built tent. Now that it is morning and the weather has loosened its grip on your throat, you figure you have to move, even though you are in a pretty bad way – you can't feel your feet and you sort of stumble even when you're just trying to roll over. Dom doesn't move at all, not even when you shake him and shove a tube of bland food into his blistered mouth.

You ease out of the tent. The sun is shining in the cold sky and the wind has trickled away to the east.

Lisa's sled is sitting at the bottom of the cliff.

You close your eyes.

You open them again.

How has she gotten down?

Pulling on your stiff boots, you stagger over, bending your head to her mouth. Her breath kisses your ear and glides around your cheek.

'The fuck?' you say.

You touch her face, then hurry back to the tent and shake your friend violently.

'Get up,' you insist.

It takes nearly ten minutes, but Dom drags himself out of dead sleep and crawls across the snow to his wife, leaving long, smooth tracks in the snow. He huddles there with his face just above hers, breathes her air and then collapses beside her on the sled, just about embracing.

You do not know what to do.

There is no way you can get them both off the mountain.

You wait for fifteen minutes, call their names and rest your hands on their heads. But you are exhausted and every second is a fading jewel, so you pack up the tent and start to flounder down the next ridge.

$\sim$

White is the colour of despair.

You know it well. For the first couple of hours the weather holds back. It watches your limp progress from a distance, mocks as though you are a bad film dribbling across its screen. Then it moves to change the channel in a mess of static snow. As you whirl around and try to strike back, the flakes dodge and titter then rush to the safety of their army of companions laid out on the ground.

There is nobody at your side and you have never felt more alone; you are shuffling centimetres down and across and the light is gone and you wish that your friends were still with you; together you could hold each other close and share the warmth, you could strive at the head of long ridges and fight back hordes of cloud, you could stand on the steps of each other, down the frowning brows of cliff and the face of the peak would be forced to let you leave without a blink; there, you would be sitting at basecamp, barren of ice and bountiful in tents and food, warmth and support, and together you would tell stories to hold the savage past at a distance, unable to hurt you anymore.

But this is useless dreaming. You are being withered and the night has flung the dark so soon; your breath is a poor and fading engine, you have wandered off the route and now you are taped to a long drift of snow that will hold you till the seasons unravel the cold. There is no prospect of seeing your friends again: Dom with his strength and wiry competence, Lisa with her humour and warmth.

Or is there?

You heave your body into the collapsed tent and wait for the malingering dawn.

⁓

In the morning you look out of the tent and it is just as you thought – the sled has slipped down the mountain again. Now you can hardly move and there is no prospect of rescue. What else is there to do?

It is time to join the others.

You creep over to Dom and Lisa and lie down with them. They are still breathing. For a few minutes you sense the silent peace of death washing over your feet, along your calves and thighs, into your guts and chest.

Then you feel a hand in your face.

'Get away,' says Dom, reaching across Lisa's shoulders. 'Get away from my wife.'

You are not sure you can speak. You cling to her a little tighter.

The hand pushes more firmly.

'I've seen you looking at her,' he says.

You shift position and the hand slips off. It forms a fist, tries to punch you.

You don't move. The warmth of Lisa's body is irresistible.

Dom tries to punch you again; this time it lands. It is weak and unpersuasive, an old man's punch, but his jacket scrapes against your frozen skin. You think about fighting back. Maybe you could push him off and lie there together with her?

You have always liked Lisa. She has a lovely face and there has always been something in the way she has flicked her hair and smiled at you across a fire.

For the first time in days you begin to feel a sense of hope.

Conglomerate

1.

They had been walking away the morning through a stretch of jaded plains that barely bothered to lift up clumps of scrub; indifferent plains that let them wander where they wanted, that channelled the broken sky between long rows of heaving mountains. Rose had been striding out the front with her peeling blue jacket warding off the prospect of rain; consulting her old-fashioned map and compass every hundred metres, comforting the paper with magnetic assurances and resting her hands on her hips as she waited for the rest of the group to catch up, her hair damp and speckled with old drips. Behind her walked Aaron with his bright blond hair balding quickly and his new boots, smooth and polished, subject to mockery by his companions and the landscape's grinding stones. Further back, Sonia, short and sturdy and able to lug boulders in her pack, and Bryony with her cantankerous enthusiasm for difficult weather and terrain, a rock-climber and former Overland Track guide who was delighted by anything out of the ordinary, no matter what obstacle it might thrust at her; they were nurses at the public hospital and obsessive photographers of beetles and peaks and vibrant shapes and colours wherever they were to be found. Then Marco, a little older; his wife with no apparent interest in getting outside and bashing her head against the fog. While he walked, she drove their two young children, both boys, to her sister's house where they played in a wilderness of rudimentary and largely percussive musical instruments you could shake, hit and blow without regard for melody or rhythm, instruments that sounded like a hailstorm heaving about a flock of failing birds, making videos for Marco to admire when he returned from the hills even as he was comparing lunches and swapping chocolates and nuts, joking about past walks and crucial tent pegs left behind in the garage with the shovels and old gloves, established territory well mapped by friendly banter on many previous occasions. There, amid all that inconsequential and perfectly happy chatter, Rose was tearing a muesli bar from its plastic sheath before moving on to sandwiches of ham and cheese and what seemed by the stains on her shirt to be a kind of tomato chutney; waiting for a lull in the showering fronts of conversation, swallowing the chunk of wholemeal bread that had been pummelled by her jaws for an unusually long time – when she finally spoke, Rose kept her eyes averted from her companions, addressing instead her fingers and her food. Perhaps it was inspired by the mountain they were felling, a shard in the south-west with many cliffs that trembled at their exposure; the risk of slipping off the rock. Strange and unfamiliar terrain. None of the safe, shattered steps and cracks of dolerite crystals or the sharp edges of quartzite; this was a rock built from fragments poorly mortared together. Unfocused and lacking clear identity. Handholds that broke apart and crumbled, surfaces that swept you off your feet. Rose had looked up at those cliffs and the blend of weather and 'well,' she started uneasily, 'do you ever think about how walking would change for you if one of us died out here?' There was a pause, and then laughter as the others refused to take her question seriously. First Bryony: 'Would be a hell of a lot quieter at night.' And Aaron, grinning at Marco: 'Guess I'd have to get a lift with some other hoon.' And while the conversation sped down a gully into the merits of various sleeping bags, then hospital overspending, then the particular shade of mud that was staining Marco's knees – was it crap mud or shit mud or possibly just mud mud – Sonia leaned forward a little, pushed her short, straggly hair out of her face, and said, 'I dunno. I really don't know how it would be.'

2.

In the dregs of the previous year Aaron and Marco had spent a day chasing high places on the Central Plateau and wondered at those species that were losing their hold and slipping off the tips of peaks as the flushed air warmed. Flowers blown away by dry mainland winds, trying vainly to sprout in the southern ice. If only the mountains were a few hundred metres higher, if only those threatened shrubs could be sown in the air and the clouds, feeding off the cold veins of water and busy minerals that circled in the atmosphere's metropolis. 'Marco,' said Aaron, shaking his head, 'Can't see them hanging on.' But what was to be done about it? Could they build great cairns or poles on the highest peaks, where the thinning vegetation might sit safely in a carefully prepared garden of native dirt like a saint cut off from the concourse of extinctions? Or perhaps a more down to earth solution. Marco suggested to Aaron: 'You know, I reckon we could at least raise some cash.' Funds to extend the shivering rooms at the botanical gardens, a broad-shouldered donation that would enable the directors to care for an old and lumbering climate that was being lost like so much megafauna, a climate that could not adapt to what had been thrown at it. That was it, they thought, that was it. And so Aaron and Marco put a proposition to their friends, to Rose and Sonia and Bryony, and they were excited at the thought of protecting those plants, of barricading the heat from their skin. To raise awareness, to give the cause a profile, the five of them walked the island from north to south, from the town of Penguin at the lip of the strait along the trail to Cradle Mountain, then all the way down the Overland Track. The heavier work over the King Williams and Denisons, bypassing the Frankland Range via a long bitumen and gravel bash along the Gordon River Road to Scotts Peak Dam, from where they took the Port Davey and South Coast Tracks to Cockle Creek. Only Aaron and Marco walked the whole span of the island; the others joined them for extended legs as they were able, using the remainder of their time to promote the challenge through busy media and online networks, crowdfunding and sponsorship. And as the weeks trudged past and donations hurried in to the island, as the local daily covered the story and kept up with their progress with photographs and maps, and as they spoke to the ABC on a satellite phone, there was a certain recognition of them as walkers in the community; not fame, but enough prominence for their names to be tuned clearly to their hobby. Their names were recognised in bushwalking circles like the author of a guidebook or a prominent peak-bagger. They were a group blending their highest ideals: getting out and enjoying the bush while working to protect it for the pleasure of others. There were many days when their wrinkled feet ached as though their bones were diverging and the arches crumbling, their backs and hips wired with fiery threads of pain. They had pressed through the early discomfort of their slack suburban muscles and arrived into true track hardiness, lean and strong, but had then stepped further into a new phase; vicious cramps, the sweat dissolving their joints. The slow, patient wear and tear needled away and sewed them a suit of weariness and strain that covered their whole bodies. The trial of rising every day and wrapping stiff socks and reeking leather boots around their protesting feet. Their stretched shorts and shirts, washed uselessly in rivulets and never really drying. Eating the same meals of oats and rice blended with thin powdery flavours. The bland wheat, the plastic cheese. Bryony, on the nineteenth day: 'Where are the hamburgers? You bastards promised me hamburgers.' Tearing down the wet tents and hoisting packs on their backs, the endless tracks laughing before them, laughing on and on. The hurtling snow, the rain and ice, the mist covering their eyes with so many palms; and yet also, the wondrous rest they found in that way of being, as though they had discovered something essential that everyone else, all around the world, was desperate to know.

How to square such sensations? The inner and outer slowly eroding, a curse on their bodies and a blessing for their minds. All five of them had walked the final leg from Melaleuca through to Cockle Creek in the far south-east, striding across the mud and the beaches, slogging through ranges and tip-toeing through rivers, swatting at mosquitos and taping up their gear; and when they finally emerged from the loose forests that swayed by the buttongrass plains and found the road waiting for them with its pale face so knowing and aware, they were certain that their steps through that final day had been lagging for a reason, that it was not truly exhaustion but rather a species of slowly-dawning reluctance. For even as they plodded past the ranger station and saw their support cars and a photographer from the paper and a spread of encouraging faces with their hands waving, even as they felt the relief and triumph in their spirits at concluding their journey – at the same time they felt a longing that sang from deep within them as though all five were being summoned to turn around, to bypass their welcome and the easy wheels back into town with its shops and restaurants and homes upon homes and plod back down the track past familiar gum leaves to walk the same routes again, this time from south to north, going back and forth like a migrating bird, feeding on what feeble sustenance they could find. Aaron and Marco, particularly, held back as the group was embraced by their family and friends. 'Want to get back out there?' Marco asked, and for a moment Aaron understood that he was perfectly serious, and he knew that he felt exactly the same way. But they were swamped by the small crowd smiling and shaking their hands, 'you did it,' everyone was saying, 'bloody fantastic' – for the walk had been completed and the money had been raised, tens of thousands of optimistic dollars, and the rooms would be built and the poor, down-trodden plants would live on. To Rose and Sonia, Bryony, Aaron and Marco, it felt that even though they had walked so far, they had in fact done nothing at all.

Everything, absolutely everything had been done to them.

3.

It could only be regarded as a tragic accident. Certainly, as the reports were later to show, the leader on the vegetation survey had led them down the wrong gully. They all looked much the same – the scrub, the huge monolithic rocks, the sky, the steep slabs of buttongrass on mud – though nothing untoward actually happened until they were back slipping down the pad itself. Wet weather had got to the rock earlier in the morning but it remained safe walking, walking that dozens of men, women and children, from five years old to eighty, enjoyed every day on tracks all over the island. Careful with every step, both hands free and ready to catch at a branch, an overhanging prickle of leaves if their feet were suddenly flung sideways. They had con-toured below the cliff-line through the boulders to the taped route that led back down to the three cars stretching out and dozing. And then Aaron had stepped on a root. It was a snow gum with hooked leaves shivering in the light breeze, and it had sent its brown roots – dark with shades of lighter brown – twisting along the ground and into the air in search of the water that was absolutely everywhere. Garden variety roots, but Aaron had done a lot of walking and the soles of his boots were bare tires with the tread sanded back and they slid against the wet root and he fell over backwards – not far, not even off the track – and someone behind him had laughed. So little blood, they said afterwards. One of their party grazed her knee on a pointed stump and it bled more than Aaron's wound. But the back of his head crashed into a fist of conglomerate that was pressing from the dirt and he slumped like a pack collapsing to the ground after a hard day's forging forward. Just a few centimetres to either side and it would have missed his head completely or been cushioned by his day pack.

The two walkers further back waited for him to shuffle up as a fantail landed on a twig that barely acknowledged its arrival. They offered mild concern. 'Aaron, are you all right mate?' Was he teasing them, taking a moment to emphasise his clumsiness, the impact of the fall? A glove on his shoulder, and then another one. 'Aaron? Mate?' Calls to the party ahead, 'Guys, get back here!' The whole group buzzed around his prone figure, a doctor pushed in to the confusion and 'Aaron, can you hear me?' she called firmly while checking his breathing and examining his pulse.

In the evening someone telephoned Rose. She was cooking a simple meal of pasta; stiff spirals lapped up the boiling water and tinned tomatoes sizzled in the frying pan with the bare minimum of onions, garlic and olive oil. She was bent over the stove, stirring more frequently than the meal really needed, as though on that cool evening it was she who needed heating, stirring away in that empty house with the television unplugged and boxed up in the cupboard under the stairs. The bare light shone in the kitchen, her fridge hummed and then the phone rang. And Rose let it ring. Stirring away at that sauce, she allowed it to ring on and on and eventually the phone shrugged and gave up trying to attract her attention. Rose reached for the colander hanging from a nail and dumped the pasta in a wad like she was trying to throw it away. She turned off the hot plates and reached to tip the draining pasta into the frying pan – it would save on washing up – when the phone gathered up its courage and tapped at her shoulder again; it rang and rang and with a sigh Rose let her wooden spoon dangle in her dinner like a slack fishing rod, flicked the heat on the pan to the lowest setting and then jogged into the living room, not bothering to turn on the light, for she could see where the phone was complaining away on the undercoated windowsill. As she picked up the handset and it began to murmur grievances in her ear, Rose was glad it was still dark in that room, for the light that peered from the kitchen seemed to have no sympathy at all for what she was hearing. Her hunger disappeared; the food she had been preparing seemed an insult. For who could eat now that Aaron would never eat again? The meal she had been slapping together was undeniably camping food, a simple set of ingredients that could be counted on one hand, heaved into packs and stewed up in the dark on low and unambitious blue flames; ideally in company, sitting together around an uneven stonehenge of rocks, logs and bunches of grass, swapping anecdotes and swigs of cheap port. Or, if the rain was pouring and breaking up the party, then boiling water, alone, in the tent's cramped vestibule, wrapped in a sleeping bag and only just poking one's nose out into the weather; the wet scrub nesting the stove, balancing it awkwardly even when it was screwed into the ground. After Rose ushered the phone into silence and replaced it on the charger, she stood there in the dark for a long time, and then she sat on the couch with her face in her hands. When she returned to the kitchen and her forgotten meal, the pasta had turned lazy and sick, and even on the low heat the sauce had dried out until it was burnt black against the pan. Rose stood there in the shrill light and she threw her ruined meal into the sink and let both the hot and cold taps rain down.

4.

In the morning, Rose met with Sonia and Bryony for an early coffee – before her work and after theirs – for the two younger women had been working late shifts at the hospital, and they explained to Rose that all through the night, as they tended to injuries and illnesses, working their backs out through the grinding hours, they had felt that somehow, they had done wrong; that they had abdicated their real duty by not being on hand to help Aaron. There had never been any plans to include them in the party, a group of volunteers surveying the spread of a rare orchid. They always found it impossible to find those tiny, private flowers when they magnified their lenses and pressed their noses close to the ground, even – especially – when they were pointed out. But still, they gritted their teeth and tore their hearts into tatters at how derelict they had been in their responsibilities; sleeping through the stupid day and working at the useless hospital, when they could have been on that trip, could have brought all their medical experience to bear and maybe, just maybe, they could have saved Aaron; at the very least given him a particle of hope. 'There was a doctor there,' said Rose, trying to comfort them. 'There was a doctor there and there was nothing she could do. It was a freak thing.' It didn't make any difference and Sonia sipped fiercely at her tea; if only she had stepped away and let the cancer patient dress his own wounds, medicate his own terrible spasms of pain and just take care of his own damn self, then she could have been on that walk with Aaron, she could have pushed the doctor aside and ministered to him and bandaged him and washed him and held him and held him and he would have ended up healthy and alive; he would have shaken his head and pulled himself together, grimaced and gotten up and felt the back of his head, checking his fingers for traces of blood, and that would have been that. Certainly he would have been grateful to her – 'thanks Doc,' he would have winked, 'but fuck that's sore' – and they would have taken a spell and snacked on a bag of cashews and then walked on and found absolutely thousands of those ridiculous tiny orchids blinking their eyes innocently in the sun.

Trammelling all through Sonia's silence like a stampede of boots over fresh snow, Bryony talked and she couldn't stop. She was furious at the sheer pointlessness of such an accident, at the members of the survey party who had been so careless as to let Aaron die. 'I can't believe it,' she said, 'I don't see how something like that could happen. Why didn't they do something? It can't be Aaron; it must be someone else. We were going to be walking to PB in the summer; jeez, he was coming over to dinner next week. What were they thinking? That fucking stupid rock.' Rose rested her hand on Bryony's arm and as she stroked away at her friend's skin, her hair felt very grey; she drew back her fingers and held that hair tightly, as though to stop it leaking from her scalp and frittering away. It seemed so brittle to the touch, and she brushed it down like she was smoothing a pile of dirty feathers. 'I just can't see why they couldn't save him,' Bryony was still insisting. 'Why wasn't someone there who knew what they were doing?' And Rose was shaking her head, gulping her strong coffee. 'Oh Bryony,' she said, 'I know,' then Sonia found a voice born deep in the pits of her body which came to her breath in the form of a small, hurt query. 'Has anyone told Marco?' Rose and Bryony tried to grasp her question. Surely Marco would have been told by someone; it was day now and the day brought these things to light. Horrendous news such as this spread like the morning fog pressing out and covering everything; no-one would be able to see anything clearly, except through the gloomy filter it forced on their eyes. Other walkers and conservationists were posting their tributes, their photographs and their grief on social media and the morning news on the radio had choked through its report. There was a sense that certain veins of the city were completely blocked up, lovers of the outdoors shocked and stricken; as they weren't whenever a tourist from Japan felt a hypothermic chill slicing through their skin, as they weren't at all when a wealthy pensioner from Sydney's heart protested and complained and then screamed on a steep section of track. This was directed at them, at someone who had laughed with them and walked with them and shared his tea and cheese, who had posted images online that others had liked and admired. Aaron had been dragged away like a warm, sunny day before a vicious storm and there was no more afternoon to linger in. He was gone, just gone, and the walkers in the city and their families and friends looked up at the bushy hills that once embraced them but now hemmed them in; eyeing their burly companions with a certain suspicion and fear, as they did for a year or two after a big fire gathered its forces and laid siege to the suburbs. The empty-handed trees maintained such blameless faces that beckoned them all to come and play; but what were those legions of eucalypts plotting? What conspiracies were being hatched below the bark? How were they uniting with the rivers and stones, the mud and the wind, against the people below? All through that pristine morning it felt like something in their world had been tugged and realigned, as though savage bears now wandered in the forests with slashing claws and teeth, bears who would creep up behind you and rip your face to pieces. Squadrons of mosquitos were armed with dengue and malaria. The snakes were spiteful and fearless. The devils were true devils and not threatened by anything. There were so many demons and ghouls that plunged a dark, stained curtain down to shroud the happiness they all felt in the bush. It was a childlike pleasure cruelly spoiled, an incident which struck at the centre of how they understood their place, their home; an eruption of the perils of elsewhere that were kept at arm's length across the strait and the oceans as the fronds of ferns shielded the view. Now those fronds were sticking in their eyes, scratching, poking and prodding. 'Open,' they were saying. 'Open up, and look. Do you see now? Nothing is fine and there is nowhere that you can hide.' But surely Marco knew? Rose clutched at the handles of her cup and upset the table with her knees. For Marco had taken his wife Angie and the boys on a walk to the Tyndalls – an accommodation that Angie had finally made, despite her concerns about the cold and discomfort in the outdoors. She had wanted to be there when Marco introduced their children to the other half of the island – that wet and green wildness. It was just for four days, four bare days, but Angie had worried and fussed and Marco had joked with them all, how she had insisted on blowing their savings on new and unnecessary gear for the boys that none of them would be able to heft up the hills; but he had laughed with a certain sympathy, for he knew it was difficult for her and he was grateful that she was willing to try, for their marriage, for their children and for him. 'Would he have reception?' Bryony asked, chewing at her nails, and Rose wondered if a call would be the right way to hurl the news against him. But she pulled her phone from her handbag and thumbed to his contact with a certain dread until his name and number glowed. She gravely pressed at her screen as though she was pushing a drastic, irrevocable button, hoping her call would be diverted straight to voicemail, hoping it would crash against the hills and peaks that separated them and be picked up by the wind and blasted out into the Tasman Sea to plunge into the deafening waves and sink to the ocean floor, never to be heard from again. As the connection inched its way across the landscape, persisting through hardships and gritting its teeth, and as Rose waited for it to clasp its hand on a distant summit, she saw her dark worries reflected in the faces of the two nurses across the table, and for a moment she was heartened. For it felt as though they were together, that the three of them would be speaking at the same time, hurrying to Marco from all sides with their arms outstretched and comforting him, holding him together, holding each other in their small chorus of grief. But then as she waited for the call to break through the layers of cloud and forest, Rose felt very alone once again, for she was the one who would have to say the awful words, the one to hear Marco's reaction, his response; it was her responsibility, she was all alone and the cafe had emptied out and the table was barren and the cups and saucers had disappeared, the napkins had fluttered away and the salt had been poured down the sink and there were no dishes clinking or cars growling on the street, it was just her, the phone and the line, so before she could find out for certain if he was waiting on the tip of a mountain where the towers could see him clearly, scrabbling for the waterproof pouch that sang away in the bottom of his pack, Rose pressed her thumb against the screen and rang off. 'He didn't pick up,' she said. 'It went straight to voicemail, just like we thought.' And she stirred at her coffee with a spoon, even though she hadn't added any sugar. They bowed their heads in a kind of unspoken prayer, worrying, wondering, till Sonia raised her eyes. 'What should we do?' she asked. 'We're off for the next three days, we've been working nights all week. We're available, I guess.' And Rose was unbearably conscious that she too would be free from any responsibilities once she had taught the morning's music classes in the primary school on the hill. There was nothing to which she had committed in the days following that couldn't be put off. She searched inside herself for courageous bones, for parts of her body that resonated brave and strong when daunting notes rang out beneath her skin, and she had to drag the question out of the very depths of her gut. 'Well do you think we should go and tell him?'

5.

As Sonia packed her gear she tried to understand how she was feeling. She had left the others toying with rough strategies at the cafe, talking more for the sake of talking than because any plans truly needed to be worked out. Their voices were thrumming in her ears like rain on an iron roof, and it seemed as though they were still walking with her, hand in hand and chattering, all the way back to her house in Mount Stuart. When she had been sitting with them at the table she had felt something of the opposite; that she had been sipping her tea all alone and by herself. The mood of mourning that swept through her system was like a drug, so powerful and overwhelming that it had confused and perhaps reversed her impressions of what was truly real.

What did this mean for her afternoon? Had day become night? She was certain that if she were to lie on her bed she would go straight to sleep, and it wasn't just the series of late shifts that was pressing her down. What did such confusions and inversions mean for the drive the following morning, for their walk going out after Marco and his family? The bush had blinked and something had shifted, and Sonia did not yet know how she felt about walking among the rocks that had betrayed them so savagely. She shoved her sleeping bag right down into the depths of her pack and then her one-person tent, her sleeping mat. What we carry, she thought, is what makes sleep possible. She rested her hand against the mattress and thought about sitting beside her pack, then lying down on the bed; but she shook her whole body and hurried out of the room, slipped into a pair of sneakers and went for a walk. She circled a series of blocks in her suburb sloping up the hill and peered into gardens at the arrangements of trees and shrubs, at the different levels of moisture, the shades of colour and varied moods that attended every house and yard, the brick and weatherboard, the magnolias and the silverbeet, the sinking decks and the sandstone barbecues; each of them a world set aside, to and for itself, as though the boarded up fences that defined their perimeters had a real and lasting meaning. She picked a red flower from one yard and set it down peacefully in the grass of another. On a corner, a lumbering mulberry tree stretched a weary branch across the footpath, green leaves shading out the grey clouds; she ripped a berry from a stem even though it wasn't anywhere near to ripe, and she popped that berry on her tongue and felt it slice across the juices of her mouth. Sonia looked up at the sky and she looked to the darker hills. When she got home, she avoided her bedroom and started tidying the disordered corners of her house, returning spatulas and plates and saucepans in the kitchen to their proper drawers and cupboards, boxing up a jigsaw she had begun putting together on the kitchen table.

She wandered down to the back of the yard, making sure that the few garden tools she kept on active service – spade, fork and secateurs – were stowed away safely from the rust. Sonia thought about oiling the door; it was important to keep busy, and so she picked up a fading can of WD40, wiped the nozzle clean of dust and sprayed the lubricant into the crevices of each hinge. The smell soaked into the air and sweetened her nostrils, and she swung the door back and forward with pleasure as though she was stroking a cat. Then Sonia carried the grimy can up to the house and sprayed the hinges on the back door which hadn't been giving her any trouble or protest at all; but it paid to be careful, to be as prepared as you possibly could be for any distress that might be thrown at you. She walked into the kitchen and sprayed the hot and cold taps, the aging coffee machine, the knives and forks of the good cutlery set that she kept in its box above the fridge. The door to the living room, and then her bedroom. She opened it wide to reach the hinges more directly and there her pack was, still waiting like a crying baby; something that could not be avoided, no matter how she tried.

∼

Bryony, after all her protests and indignation, found that she couldn't stop weeping; so much tea tree that she couldn't push through and sleet that she couldn't laugh off. She couldn't bear the bus, so hurried home on sore feet and washed her face, washed her boots and her gaiters and her coat, washed a set of thermals and an extra pair of socks and it all came up so clean. Her tanned reflection in the bathroom mirror fogged over – the cool sense of walking in wet clouds – and she worried that her miserable, grieving mood would usher in the grey weather that was building; that she would be a fifth columnist, responsible for unlocking the gate and letting in the drizzle and the rain, calling it all down on them in a kind of sympathy as they clambered on to the ridges. Perhaps they would miss Marco in the mist, pass within a few paces and never see the colour of his coat; she wasn't sure, as she cried, whether this was a good or bad thing. Brief, consoling messages appeared on her phone, but she couldn't look at them; she didn't want to know. Photographs on Facebook, lengthy, appreciative messages of sadness and regret, images of Aaron striking shy poses on stone seats and walking up buttongrass hills. What was he doing there? She didn't want to see him there. Bryony left her phone in her bedroom and sat down on her couch. She tried to pull a novel from her shelf to read in the dim light, but her eyes were unfocused, as though she was reading at the wrong scale, tuned in to pages as a whole and unable to see the detail of blurred words or follow any narrative they might be offering to her. She began laying out a pack of cards, as though she was already caught inside her tent by foul weather battering against the fly. A game of solitaire, seven columns with their company of faces cast down, a graph lining the table showing an increase in some property, a growth, even as her weeping was easing up. Many times, worn out and battered after a long day shepherding novice walkers through the national park, she had turned to such cards as a careless consolation, and she had kept up the habit when she graduated to nursing. Every card she dealt was like a footstep; but such tiny steps did not convince her she was getting very far. A waltz with the spare cards, one-two-three, one-two-three; filling gaps and transferring whole stacks, modifying the rules as she proceeded when the game began to strangle her attempts and play dirty. The ambiguities of blank columns and what could be shifted there; mixing up the spare cards and filching a jack out of order. Because really, the important thing was to keep the game going for as long as she possibly could, to bring every card under its proper king and queen. To just make the whole damn thing work out.

~

The clamour of the news. Rose had turned down the radio in the car; the hourly bulletins she seemed always to be catching between errands – the same refugee boat overturning in the Mediterranean with the same thirty-five people missing, the same boilover in the tennis overnight with the same gracious platitudes offered by the young victor – and the same short and utterly inadequate report about a bushwalker who had been killed in the central highlands, the same meagre and useless sixty-three words, summarising it down to nothing. The first time she had heard it announced, Rose experienced a kind of gratification; the acknowledgement that this event, her event, was significant enough to be broadcast, known and felt by the wider community. But with the second and third and fourth repeats – as she stocked up on dehydrated food and another bottle of metho – it had begun to feel like a kind of routine, a senseless mantra or form of white noise; that there was a well-ordered box into which everyone listening would be filing the incident. A sombre note pealing in their minds, and then a question: did we know him, or did we know someone who did? No? Still, it was very sad, wasn't it? Or perhaps she was wrong. Perhaps everyone was feeling just as she was, a horrible, rending shock that this could have happened to a walker like Aaron. The people of the town struck silent, without a glib cliché or superior explanation to offer, not even nodding or shaking their heads. 'That's terrible. That's awful. Think of his family and friends.' Aaron was such a good, strong bushwalker. He had walked the state from north to south, and then the island had found a new direction for him and ushered him all the way down. As the radio droned on Rose grew impatient – the poverty of words to explain anything at all – so she muted its assured tones. When she got home and stuffed the food she had bought into a yellow drybag and leaned it against her pack, she broke her habit of listening to the evening news and went to bed very early with the twilight still huddling in her bedroom. In the morning, she woke in the dark to eat a quick breakfast of toast and coffee. She threw her gear in the back of the hefty four-wheel drive, and as she drove to pick up Bryony and Sonia, sitting outside their homes on low brick fences, Rose ignored the headlines blaring from their stands outside the newsagencies as though they were a kind of false prophet, proclaiming messages that were not so much inaccurate as oversimplified in every way that mattered. The only thing that she could do was set her eyes against them.

6.

Rose, without thinking, had parked right next to Marco's van. They stood in the small carpark near the gate, unloaded their packs and let them crash against the gravel with the wet dust clinging. The three women pursued their rituals: checked their zips for gear they worried about forgetting, confirmed maps and torches; adapted their layered clothes for the conditions and removed synthetic jackets – for though there was drizzle smearing the air, the day was muggy and humid, thick with heat. They stepped into stiff-necked boots and bandaged up their legs with gaiters. Ate their first muesli bars and bananas. Tinkled keys in the tops of their packs – it was time to make for the track head. So many customs and routines. A protection and a comfort, like every step; the talisman of forward movement. A solemn duty and a pilgrimage; they were envoys carrying crucial news across dangerous terrain. Rose signed her name in the logbook, checking and confirming the route that Marco and his family were planning to follow. Each of them had a piece of gear that they would normally leave in the cupboards at home: a GPS, an extra thermal top, two or three triangular bandages. It didn't feel that they were trespassing into enemy territory so much as entering a kind of no-mans land, emptied of personal imprints and considerations; a fraternity of trees that was both threatening and charming. And even though that landscape, as they strode up the steep, pebbly trail, was not a completely hostile power, beating, torturing, hanging and shooting them for daring to impose their bodies on its boulders, all three women kept their heads hooded and bent low, making no eye contact with the sleeping conglomerate slabs. They backed away from any altercation, cameras buried in the bottoms of their packs, only brought out at times because changing their liturgy would have been more troubling. The ridges ahead of them were empty of red and orange figures, but it would only take one or two frames and the clouds would clear and there they might be, walking inexorably towards them. Could it be, the women wondered, that they already knew about it? Perhaps the family had climbed up to the tip of Geike, removed their phones and checked the cricket score, uploaded a picture of the whole family laughing and triumphant, the ranges waving behind them, and then noticed on the feeds another photo, and then another; so many photos of Aaron. Or they could have stopped for a friendly chat with another walker. 'Where are you guys headed to?' 'Isn't it great country?' 'Magnificent. I could live up here, even through the winter.' Updates on the weather, and then, as they were running out of conversational steam: 'Terrible thing. Did you hear the news yesterday?' And Marco would be curious. Had there been another flood on the mainland or a fire devastating the peninsula? 'The news?' he would have asked. Were they now rushing along the plateau with stiff, heartbroken faces, the boys growing up into the dark moods of their parents? Angie shaken, all her fears confirmed. How could she ever go into the wilds again, how could she let the boys, how could she risk the boys, how could she even let Marco? Yet giving no voice to her concerns, just striding over the top of her small blisters and checking her husband's face for any signs of how he might need her to respond to him in such a dark hour. To let him have his space, or to whisper beside his steps: was he okay, was there anything at all that he wanted to talk about? More likely they would still be ignorant and happy, snoozing in their sleeping bags, Marco frying up some bacon to meet the eggs he had boiled several days before, a cup of strong tea in his hand; but just starting to think that with the gloomy weather it wasn't worthwhile staying much longer. But also that there was no reason to rush, it wasn't cold and it was cosy in the tents, and there was still another heavy bag of food to plug through, and the dog was being looked after till Thursday. And then, here was Rose walking out of the cloud, her face tired, and Sonia and Bryony too. What a lovely surprise! Cup of tea? Bit of bacon, there's plenty to go around? No? Is something wrong? All of these possibilities cycled through their minds as they climbed past the shelves of rock and over the lip of the plateau, their shoulders aching, breath forced; the sudden view expanding to other mountains and valleys, the still light wind unimpeded and cooling their sweaty skin as they pedalled their legs onward, quicker now. No lingering or chatting, as though they were out to rescue a lost bushwalker or a climber with a broken leg; and perhaps they were, though the victim didn't yet know it. 'Do you think ...' started Sonia, and then stopped as her companions turned and waited for her to continue. 'Oh, nothing, it's nothing,' she said, but they gave their full attention as she let the implications of her thought spiral out; that there must have been a party like theirs that had readied themselves to go and get Aaron, to save Aaron, and she knew, she had a sense how they must have been feeling as they packed their professionalism and drove as close as they could before striding up through the forests where he had fallen... and Sonia saw there was no consolation to be had in that thought. But the weight of Rose and Bryony's considering faces was a burden that could only be lightened with her speech, and so: 'Do you reckon we'll find them today?' she asked. 'I hope we find them today, I don't think I could bear a night out without having told them. I'd prefer to walk all through the night.' Rose studied her. 'I think we'll find them today, judging by their walk outline,' she replied. And Sonia nodded, content to let the moment pass. The tears pooled once more in Bryony's eyes and there was nothing she could do to drain them but keep on moving. Sonia's question brought the purpose of their walk to the forefront of their minds, a purpose that had been put aside through the sheer exertion of scrambling up the mountain's slope, and Rose asked herself again how they could pass on such drastic news, how could they invite Marco to join this transformed world where Aaron was a person no longer, a parallel world that was as colourless as the flat sink of sky above them? As the morning passed the baton to the early afternoon and the women approached Lake Tyndall across the high native grasslands, they saw two licks of orange paint through a gap in the shifting fog. 'God! Fuck!' said Sonia, as if reality had suddenly landed in her pack like an extra ten kilos of gear – and they looked across at the tents, and for the first time since entering that new and strange bush they felt a real kind of fear, one that broke the boundaries of the place they were traveling through; and they were strangely tentative as they walked on, as if the ground was exposed on every side and covered by faithless ice. They couldn't take their eyes off the tents for fear that if they weren't attentive, if they let their task get away from them at the final hurdle, a figure might emerge and run down the steep decline to the lakes on the eastern side to dodge their grim news. As they approached their stride grew faster, as if by consensus to get it over and done with; they almost jogged past the wizened patches of olive scrub decked in light flowers. There were no sounds or signs of movement and when they stepped into the margins of the tiny village, they stopped and were struck dumb by the absence of anyone at all. They couldn't discharge their duty. They had been left hanging by the silence, as though they had stepped into space from a massive drop but hadn't yet fallen. 'Hello?' said Rose to the tents, tapping the nearest one. A scattering of cooking gear lay in a half-open vestibule, mugs, a Trangia – but nobody was sitting there to welcome them with a hot drink. 'Must have gone for a day walk,' said Rose, swinging a leg back and forth, as though searching for something to kick. 'A bloody day walk.' She dropped her pack and grabbed a box of matches. Checked the levels of fuel and got Marco's stove going. 'Geike or Tyndall?' She put the water on and waited for her friends to join her. 'We should set up camp, anyway,' she suggested. And so as the water shook itself and started to boil, Rose, Bryony and Sonia pitched their tents, breaking with convention by huddling them together like the rooms of one lone house with all the storm guys linking arms, then they settled down on patches of uneven rock to wait, ready for the sound of children laughing, for a booming yell – 'hello!' as Marco recognised the tents – for the moment when all three of them would have to stand up together and shake out their cramping legs. Perhaps they would walk out into the drizzle and stride up towards Marco and his family, and he would pick up the pace, bounding cheerily down the slope as his sons and wife proceeded sensibly and cautiously, and all too quickly the distance would close and they would be mingling greetings, a clash of warm and cool fronts creating a strange disturbance as they hugged and trembled and spoke. Or perhaps they would wait as the hum of voices grew closer, slowly resolving into four separate people. They would sit there fiddling with their mugs and fingers, saying nothing, just staring at the scattered pink and white stones, until Marco appeared in the space between the tents and let the mess of grey clouds in.

We Are All Superman

We are all Superman. It's great! When the world needs saving we zip to a phone box and get changed into our tights and capes as quickly as we can. There aren't so many boxes these days so we have to queue, and it's kind of creepy that you can see right in, but we get used to it and, if we're at home, we figure that there's no *written* rule and so we just get changed in the bedroom and get out there to save the world as quickly as possible. We grab the evil genius who is plotting against the world, grip his wrist and frown with determination as we deliver him to the authorities. And maybe we will push him through a fucking wall. Or dangle him off the edge of a building by an ankle.

Well. The one who gets there first can do all that. The rest of us just kind of stand there with arms folded and chests filling out our suits, then we cheer and follow behind in a long sky-parade of blue. We whistle mighty tunes and swish our capes about and stare at passing eagles like: 'back off, this is *our* sky,' and we hurry the evil genius to the authorities. Medals are handed out until the city runs out of medals again and then we go back to business, waiting for the next crisis to strike.

We get on pretty well, although some of us long for the old days when we were sure to at least grasp an evil limb. But there are counselling sessions and a union and once a year we take holidays in Noosa and have a sort of convention with speakers and seminars, though mostly we are just there to sip cocktails and stretch out our muscles on the beach.

The only thing we ever squabble about is Lois. See, we are all Superman, but there is still only one Lois, and this is even worse than the thing with the criminals, because while you know that an evil genius is going to threaten the world maybe three times a day – and the law of averages says that once every few years you'll be the one who hands him over to the authorities – Lois mostly just likes one of us at any time, and this is a problem. Right now she is keen on the Superman from downtown with the *dark* hair, and all of us just sort of want to punch him in the face, but that would undercut the whole business, so when we meet at the convention we just smile at him and say 'Hey Clark, how's it going?' and he grins and says 'fine, you know. Actually, really good. Great.' We smile at him too, and when we're busy trying to save the world there's an understanding that you kind of shoulder him away from the main action, because if he got an evil genius who was looking to destroy the world *as well* then that would be the fucking worst.

Today, though, is good, because it is Saturday, and on Saturdays an evil genius goes for Lois. When an evil genius goes for Lois she isn't so fussy about which embrace she ends up in and so this is our chance. When the call comes I take straight off for the centre of town. Lois is balanced on the end of a long, yellow crane with a bomb bound up in her hair and tarantulas poised on her shoulders. There is a gun in her hand that she has pointed to her own head, and I am the first, I am the first! I'll feel her slim warmth trusting my power, the sun gleaming on our skin. Perhaps she will cast that Clark aside and tonight we will eat at the Korean place near the docks; we will hold hands for the first time and dream our way home through the settling streets. I look around for the evil genius to disable the bomb and stand down the spiders, to order him to tell Lois to take that gun out of her hand, but he is nowhere to be seen. Has he already run away? I'm very strong and intimidating. My muscles are like iron. I fly up next to Lois. She gazes at me in fear and despair. I reach up to slip the bomb from her hair and shield it with my body but she flinches, cocks the gun and closes her eyes.

'Don't come any closer,' she says. 'Please… don't come any closer.'

It's All Happening Here

I called her in the middle of the night and waited for her to answer
with a voice that I didn't know and hadn't heard in years, a voice from
a phone book or a gentle collision in the street, and the dark inside
was strong and the grass outside was weeping with dew while a light
frost had honed its edge on the corners of the lawn in the shadow of
the night now night, and there in my hand was an old-fangled phone
with its dirt-cream body like a shack-town sink and its dial all hurried and laboured. She was propping up a gaggle of galleries in Berlin
with her paint-smeared hands and firm euros and I remembered how
she had wanted to be a geologist, to stir up stones and bake her hands
on golden sand, to measure the tension in loping hills; but there she
was framing the souls of young fools. And could it be that she had
sunk to the pits of creativity herself, mining pigments that swirled
with new currents and shades? No, just a clipboard refuge for her
parade of blond artists with their t-shirts and tagged chests. There
was a photograph of her on the gallery's website at an opening with a
glass of wine, looking uncertain and committed; a pair of scissors in
her other hand, as though she was going to cut a ribbon or trim the
meadows of unruly hair that topped the hills around her. When she
looked at me from this photograph, she did not know who I was. She
shrugged and stared from my screen. She snatched at her primary
school photographs, at forgotten badminton tournaments. The frost
was creeping up, catching and assimilating the dew, and I watched
from the chilled window as it slid across the lawn like a tide of aching,
and I tapped on the window and tapped at the screen and she was
puzzled; the smile creeping through her sealed face hinted at a tactful
attempt to laugh me off, to return my grasping eyes to the backwa-
ters and the colonies and expel me from reaching out for whatever it

was I had lost. I rapped harder on the screen to wake her up, yelled her name, but her image remained silent. In the end I had to call her, taking firm hold of the gallery's number and waiting till the middle of the night – a slow time in her northern afternoon with the sun lolling by the windows and lunch stretching out in her system.

She would answer the phone in German, and I did not speak German. There was a click in the earpiece. There was a whirring.

And then the voice of Tony Greig was at the end of the line. And it seemed so confusing and wrong, for instead of exclaiming, 'he's blazed that one through the off-side field…go and fetch that!' he said, 'good afternoon,' in his accented English, 'this is the Kottbusser Gallery, Tony Greig speaking,' and it felt as though his voice had been drastically tamed, as though all the energy and exuberance had been drained from his throat. At first I didn't know what to say. I wondered what had happened to his heart attack and death and I stared out the window with the phone in my hand as the frost crept up and sent the stairs slipping all over one another so they fell in a jumble at the bottom of the deck, and the ice slinked on as the deck tried to keep its own feet, and 'hello?' said Tony Greig once more, 'who's there?' while he should have been bursting with, 'it's miles in the air… it's a wonderful catch! What a catch!' And so the silence stretched out, clasping its hands and shaking its head. But before he could tuck the phone back in its bed I offered, wary and uneasy, my own version of 'hello,' and even though I knew that it had to be the Kottbusser Gallery, and that Tony Greig himself, when he answered the phone, had directly confirmed it, I asked him, 'is this the Kottbusser Gallery?' And Tony Greig informed me politely that yes, it was indeed the Kottbusser Gallery, was there any way in which he could be of assistance? Did I wish to enquire about a slab of scribbled wall or a new unstable bridge? Was I hoping to speak to someone in particular? And so I stared at that lonely image and thought to offer up her name, and then began to second, third and fourth guess myself, until my mind was as spiralled and confused as the ancient phone's cord, until the only fact that was clear to me was that while I had a species of longing for her, I could not be certain that I longed for her voice, as such; but how much I missed the voice of Tony Greig! So even though he was offering simple, everyday conversation, the mere presence of his voice comforted me more than I could say, and as the frost snuck up and glided under the front door, peering left and right, locking its gaze on my bare feet and up along my shins and my thighs, all the way up to my shivering chest and my wan face pale in the night's lost light, 'well,' I said, 'Tony Greig, I was actually hoping to talk to you.'

Landscape within Landscapes

'Around him stretched the rolling plains of his own land.'
Norstrilia, Cordwainer Smith

'First published by Norstrilia Press 1982'
Imprint Page from *The Plains,* Gerald Murnane

Did the useless man find some plains of his own, two sets slung by searing slopes, all those welcome hills like scrubby sheep leaning on their blistered sides?

He did.

Had it been so many as fifteen thousand years since the glaciers startled that landscape with deep groans?

He did not think that it could have been so distant, even though the layers and piles of echoes had long dissolved in the wind stirring sounds throughout the valley – unless the wind itself was a kind of dissipated echo, continuing its rebounding and recoiling. There was ice in that wind: ruthless ice that struck with the southerly blast.

~

The useless man's presumptions had brought him to a camp court nestled in a thatch of scrub, a hairline of dark tea-tree lining the river that creviced the plains. He wasn't at all certain whether he'd been summoned directly, or if the call had been implicit in the track's own stride as it sleeved the shoulders of the ranges; as though the landscape itself had bowed, presenting an invitation, soliciting him through the mud and buttoned grass to sit under the judgement of three souls hunched on stiff seats of quartz; stones grazed smooth by the river's song, dragged below burnt banksias with their sooty, silent rattles.

Was it a crime, a trespass that had slung him at their feet? The useless man had come to write a book of the valleys and peaks that would cage their essence, a book that would carry their wild beating to the cities on the coast. He would type with confident steps. He would map the earth with fumbling words and splatter his pages with squalls. And perhaps, he had thought, there was a certain immortality to be gained while shearing the slopes with his boots and squatting across the whole of such plains; not the misbound eternities of title pages but a timelessness swept up, breathed and exhaled.

Shaky ambitions pursued with blunt-faced determination.

$\sim$

Perhaps it was the limping sun's gaze as it hid to the north, or a change in the timbre of the voices that filtered through the ripples and rapids of the river, but the useless man was lifted from his tussock. He surged through the knee-deep mud before wading into the water; as he entered the judges' wild garden, he was asked to sit on a thick branch that flowed flat before ranging up steeply, as though the roots had sucked on veins of gold. There he slumped, lingering his gaze on their firm faces: the judges who could rip such faithless life from his fingertips and bury his body in the silty plains.

The first judge was a man with hardwood in his muscles and dark, red ore in his throat; he had stripped these elements from the mountains and plains around him, the density of his bones drawing the minerals from below the surface to rest in his waiting palms – the land offering its tithe. 'Do you understand me?' the judge asked. 'For if you don't understand me, then how can you speak to me? And if you can't speak to me then how can you speak to others of this landscape?'

The useless man had no answer to that question.

'I can see your feet,' the first judge continued. He pointed to the scraps of mud tucked in the bolt-holes of the useless man's boots. 'This mud is the glue that grips the earth together. It cups the creeks and tapes the scrub to stone; it is distilled from the country, a blend of water and the earth that mingles the weather with the ground. Do you curse this mud,' he asked, 'sidling it as a coward, or do you trudge straight through and drown your blind steps? Would you bury yourself in this mud, your body beneath its clotted skin?'

The sun leaked through the scrub ceiling.

The second judge coughed.

The useless man flicked his fearful eyes to where she waited on her stone; this judge who could ease across the jagged country, as though the landscape had filled its valleys and flattened every hill and mountain, levelling the rough and ragged ground before her even as the views whirred left and right.

She contended that the first judge's notions of mud were no vision or theory of the whole. 'But your language of clotting is revelatory,' she observed, 'for that quagmire which you worship is the land's blood, and there is a whole body built upon this blood that doesn't care whether this fool chooses to dip his toes.'

And despite her insult the useless man was filled with flimsy hope; for if there was dissension among the judges his chances might stumble home. He looked trustingly at the woman, at her waterproof skin and granite feet, at the camp that she had set high in the trees, for the view, he thought – she too must be searching for a sincere view, even in her sleep!

But her following words cast him off a cliff; she agreed with the first judge about the importance of the land's speech. 'Which is why,' she said, 'his behaviour with the grass and the trees and the scrub is more imperative, for the flora is the voice of the land. And I wonder, can he hear it as they mutter and sway in the breeze?'

And then as the tendrils of wind slipped into the grove and the clouds darkened the light, she aimed her questions at the useless man more directly. 'Do you push through the deepest bauera and cutting grass and listen as they rustle their voices? Do you climb up to the crowns of sassafras and myrtle and place your earlobes against the tips of their leaves? Do you stand solid with them, arm to branch, to be cremated as the fires sweep their leaves to silence and their bodies to the night?'

The useless man thought to mumble warily that he had shaken hands with any scrub that offered itself to him, that they had even embraced and lain down together, and 'well then,' she said, and he could imagine her standing as her own pillar among the parades of high columns, 'what has the land got to say?'

And he was silenced by her demand, with not a word to offer in his defence. For all the odours of mounting peat, the metallic chiming of rosellas and the discordant contests in currawong songs, for all his late-night gazing at the choir of stars that hymned across the sky, he was left scrabbling in his own mind. He had nothing to share with the judges or the spread of souls locked at the borders, in the cities and towns. And there was indeed no purpose to his efforts or his wandering. He had no right to the forests; he was a deluded mule, a bastard offspring of town and bush that could give birth to nothing at all.

~

The final judge, an old man with his eyes slammed shut and his hands almost covering his ears and the wings of goshawks blocking up his face with white beard, began laughing, and his laugh was like the scattering of droplets or feathers. He was a judge who painted the landscape in his mind and his mind on the landscape; and as his mirth finally subsided he corrected the second speaker, arguing that all those writhing flowers were not the voice of the land, but of the wind.

66

'And anyone who listens to the wind so closely is a fool,' he muttered from the corners of his lips. The green trees and shrubs, he continued, as the air grew thick and unbalanced, were the land's hair, less vital even than the blood. To see into the land required vision without eyes, and to speak of the land required a voice without a tongue. The judge focused his eyelids on the useless man's trembling form, and though he spoke no further words, the useless man heard questions singing in his hollow mind. *Can you hear the land? And yourself, do you have anything to say?*

And he stared at the third judge, not believing that he could offer any answer. His cocky invasion had left him mute. He had written no book to encapsulate all of those plains that lay in the midst of mountains.

And so he prepared to accept what was to come. He leaned his neck towards their sentence, and as he bowed before the judges there were multiplied in his memory glimpses of many selves, self-assured and meek, selves proud and humble, selves cunning and artless, careless and dutiful, wise and foolish, a spectrum of identities and personalities that shadowed his whole and complete person; and while he did not feel that he was any of those selves, and he wished that only their corrupt, shameful and impotent manifestations would be forced under the blows to come, each appeared to have a toe-hold in his identity that was impossible to dislodge.

He would die, he was sure, for his impertinence.

But before any of those present could further plead or weigh, appeal or condemn, before his judges could utter their verdict and carry out his execution, the sky itself boomed above them with a compelling voice and a storm of rain leapt from the clouds and dashed itself hard against them in the narrow clearing, and the noise and the pressure of the rain overcame their hearing as they stared up and around at the tumult of shattering sky. As the water gathered together and met in sudden puddles, as it glistened down the banks to swell the rising rivulet that was splaying its body across the stony shore, as it dripped from the leaves' taps and trickled down trees and his jacket and his pack, peering and ducking between canvas gaps and, above all, as it poured down his face and the faces of his judges; how their cheeks ran and ran with the urgent messages of new rivers!

And perhaps, he thought, this was as close as the land could come to weeping.

The Eradication Program

we were driven by a violent storm to the north-west of Van Diemen's Land…
I attempted to rise, but was not able to stir: for, as I happened to lie on my back,
I found my arms and legs were strongly fastened on each side to the ground; and
my hair, which was long and thick, tied down in the same manner.
Jonathan Swift, *Gulliver's Travels*

The Royal Company Islands, until expunged at the instigation of the
[Australasian Ornithologists'] union, appeared on the charts and maps as
occurring approximately 500 miles S.S.W. of Tasmania.
Letter from AH Mattingley, Hon. Sec. AOU, to
The Argus, Friday 13th August 1909

We have been eradicating the main island of the Royal Company, trudging through the snow with dense, damp boots. Soaked woollen socks chill our feet whenever we stop to rest, our arses shaped against icy, tussock-grass stools. Hurried slurps from drink bottles, scroggin spilling from plastic pockets open to our fingers and the absolute westerlies. It should be a night to pile into the cabin, hang our clothes from the cords criss-crossing the empty heights. To crowd the coal in the pot-belly and linger, staring, as though the fire were more than a glow shifting at the cracks in the door, the sleet stowed away in folds, on the top of packs, brushed into corners, darkening the floor. I should be able to laugh with them, to join them scrounging from the stores shipped down from Sullivans Cove: the mouldering blue, salmon offcuts and malty export stout.

But the small man from Mildendo is laughing again. His mockery flows uphill to the other men gathered around the stove, smothering the air with boasts and greasy hair; the smell of ham and flaccid beans. The redhead from Kaoota flicks a coal scat towards me. It grazes my cheek darkly as I sit by the cold square, condensation fogging the glass and blurring the beleaguered scrub outside. Bored cheers and the Lilliputian claps once, twice, as Kaoota's face flushes. He has a way, this man, of gathering our company and trickling through the crevices in their characters and saturating them with his bile. They are ready at his cue for quiet, bunched nastiness – or for grabbing my arms like an unruly drunk and thrusting me from their hut.

Now his voice lifts and curves round the bunks shadowed in the low light. 'He won't even tread on an ant. But his uncle, right? So here he is. None of that here though, mate.'

He must have noticed my eyes following the trail of common ants imported from the north, the way I step my path carefully to avoid theirs. Maree, I remember you loved the crawling insects that itched our arms and legs on slumping beds, that haunted the huts spread across our islands, tripping behind the walls like mice, soldiering along tracks built from their bodies; rough-housing the crumbs that dripped from our mouths to the warped planks paving the table. We would sit and watch them, holding hands as you built new bridges for them to tackle with their burdens. You would call them fellow island-ers; lucky as we were to live in such tenuous landscapes.

The Lilliputian is rubbing the sludge drying on his mauled plate of beans against his chin. The dark-haired bloke, Wynyard, with the letters, with the wife, punches his city mate Howrah in the side, and snorts. The small man's cheeks and the upper parts of his neck are now spread with the mess; a sarcastic dab on the tip of his nose. He begins to jabber nonsense, waving his arms like an ape, and the main-landers part-mirror his movements. His babble jumps in small rapids back to human speech. 'Well,' he finishes, 'time you were gone, yes?'

The men glint against me as I lay my eyes steadily against the bunks. Why not scratch my face and let the virus that has ploughed my skin fall down to rest on the mattresses? I know what that will mean for myself and the other locals they might encounter after a heavy night on the Lark. The small man reads me too well; I have passed dark thoughts across the hut. I try to turn back the seconds, suggest that he is right, it's time I leave. 'No,' he says, 'not yet.' Thinks a moment, a smile crafting his lips. 'Was hoping you might explain what that was about today.'

The ledge. We have been eradicating together for two, nearly three months. The job was completed weeks ago on the smaller archipelago speckling the nearby sea, using careful navigation with the compass, chart and the precise instruments of cartography that the small man locks in his own palms, spilling the soil into the sea and making the islands vanish. We map them and they disappear. The islets were less burdensome and we dealt with their coastlines, the sharpened rocks knifing from the tidal plains, rolled stones reeling at our feet. The guano that painted shorelines in white, foul sand. But the task has lengthened as we have circled the southern contours of the higher hills, staring down at the piecemeal hamlet huddled in the cove. Every step around my village's slipshod homes has gathered further weight. Maree, do you remember when we met on that ledge carved in the crumbling quarry stone? Falling together on our backs as the evening drank on, watching the stars bedding down? You said you could see them moving if you watched carefully enough, and I tried to find their trail marked against the night sky. 'Look, watch,' you said. 'It's like the long grass or the waves dragging specks of stone to sea.'

'Don't look too closely,' I had replied. 'You can navigate by the stars.'

I was remembering that pale autumn night when I carefully side-stepped the ledge on the afternoon's grinding shift.

'Long day,' I say, collecting my makeshift tarp, my sleeping bag and the gear spilling from my well-thumbed pack. 'I thought you blokes might want to hit the sack.'

The man from Mildendo is shaking his head. 'No mate, we're all ears here. See, the thing is, you've done it before.' Licking at his filthy hands. 'Didn't bring it up, just wanted to be sure. On the small island, near the busted jetty. Wynyard here saw you, [Wynyard nods ravenously] he pointed it out, but I wanted to check it myself. Ogled on you something special.'

It had been my grandfather's jetty. He'd tried to run sheep on a small outcrop barely stained with grass, a tiny, water-fenced paddock for three poor beasts dinghied across on a calm day. The makeshift pier was constructed from rocks and strips of rare, scavenged timber. They barely lasted a year on the rough surface; the jetty, pounded by the swell and children throwing rocks from the main island's beach, became arthritic.

I have been careful, there have been dozens of times when I have shifted my line across the slopes to preserve something precious in the landscape – but not wary enough, as my diversions have been noted. But it is miserable to watch it all go.

The small man is searching the table. He scrabbles in the wrappings, uncovering matches and spoons, tries to keep his movements deliberate. He finds a knife amongst the rubble, takes his time with it, scraping its edge against the melting pot-belly, testing the heat with his thumb. 'Well,' he says, 'if you do that again, won't be no escaping, fuckwit uncle or no. Was brought in here to do a job that you backwater inbreds couldn't manage. But I will.'

His four followers crackle into laughter and the skinny one from Nubeena throws in, 'What, never even been to Tassie, have you? Wouldn't know real land if it came up and slapped you in the balls. No wonder you sticks need some like expertise.'

He's right. Apart from these limpets on the ocean's skin, the only land I've stepped on was a forced berth. An extended fishing trip in the north-west with my cousins; savage weather sent us racing for a lee shore and we harboured in a rough cove on the south-east shore of Blefuscu. I can't help wondering if somehow, gossiping in the sparse pub leaning by the cove's pier, the small man could have heard the story; if this could be a component of his hostility.

But his is not a rare prejudice. They roar, in Hobart, at our hopelessness, our isolation. Whipping boys in turn, we let them tread us away, impressing wider admiralties with their maps and charts. When a mess they have made runs wild, they step in with their hands and their proud wallets, dropping in parties of trappers to eliminate the cats, the rabbits and the seabird-scouring rats as they did on that privileged easterly island, Macquarie. Creatures they originally welcomed with open arms and ushered on to a feral southern ark were hunted and baited, shot and sunk. The native flora unfurled its leaves; all that regrowth on the pebbled scree, and pampered penguins lolling on chilled rocks. And now here the mainlanders spend their efforts; busy making whole islands vanish.

I continue getting my camp together in silence. The infection had first appeared six days ago; the red sores jumped from my neck and spread, cancelling out my skin and any prospects I might have had of redeeming myself with the other men. When the rash appeared on our fourth night working the main island, Kaoota, the redhead piece of work, looked repulsed. 'What you been doing with your face? Your customs here, still trying to work them out. What do you reckon boys? Up home, you know what we'd say.' He searched out the eyes of his compatriots. 'Don't know if you can access that here. Maybe you get postcards down at the jetty?'

The Lilliputian had laughed to consolidate his role, but wasn't ready to tap out of tormenting, to let others take the initiative. He had asserted himself seriously, pragmatically. 'See, but we have a job here, can't have the lot of you down with faces like that. Mind, wouldn't accuse any of you ugly buggers. Just keep him off us, we'll be right.'

And so I walked separately, just within the parameters of my transect line, and camped lonely on the sides of yellowed hills, in lush green valleys with megaherbs swelling all around me. But these brief hours where they tolerate my germs are a greater plague than any solitary days trudging, or shivering in my rough, improvised tent. 'Now,' I say, 'no worries. Nothing fellas. Gonna crash.'

I step through the field of forces cast among them, their lines of presence and potential, to let me go freely or lift a heavy boot. Unmolested, I scurry outside to join the begging foliage.

∼

Every half hour I wake and sense the icy, biting blanket until light penetrates and I come to, drifting in and out as the brightening noise persists with its shaking. The strident cold; stiff fingers and toes background sleep like the persistent memory of chapped dreams. I stretch, rattle myself in my clothes, loosen the packed grime, and reach over to pound my boots into flexibility. The sound thuds across the valley like heavy-bodied footsteps. Matches and numb fingers; a metho-flavoured cigarette.

There is a light mist in the air, a clinging wetness resting from the droving wind that herds it to the hilltops, then down the slope again to ocean. We have been lurking in the gullies overnight where tiny rivulets are open, bereft of overhanging scrub and pouring down runnels in the hills. Leaves with wide, blank faces; the native cabbage wonders how it has ended up here and awkward rocks summit the slopes. As I wait for the water to boil I reach down to a cushion plant and wipe my hands against its dense flesh. The birds are up today. I'm reminded again that we are close to breaking waves, the calls of petrels and prions arcing above the easterly cliffs, dropping back to singsong waves, fluid nests moulded around their peddling feet.

The water is getting up on its haunches. I toss it a rough handful of tea leaves and wait for the strong beast to stew. It's not so bad out here; the hut isn't insulated, just a pile of boards and corrugated iron, not much warmer than my camp. Dark, though, grim even in the height of a glorious day that distends the early morning for snoring men. When I decide the tea is ready, I fill my scratched plastic cup, splashing the sides and the firm dirt ground, warm my hands and face. One of the group appears at the door, pisses off the deck. Thinks to say something, but in the absence of mates decides to save it for later. Others appear and go through their waking motions. I let them keep to themselves, finish the tea and pack my gear quickly; there'll be enough time for another cup and perhaps a warm, powdery porridge if they let the minutes trickle on.

There's a faint suggestion of sun in a dispersed glow to the east; when we finally move, the glimmering has strengthened and shrunk. Packs gripping our backs, we lurch towards the sea, measuring, checking and annotating maps. We are a staggering line of six. The small man occupies a central lane, the rest of us stepped out at ten metre intervals, confirming mathematically, scientifically, that there is no land there and continuing the slow eradication. There is now a light breeze on my face that feels like a rebuke, but I continue pacing, letting the dirt, the spears of grass, the frosted droplets evaporate behind me.

I should have known that trouble was on the cards. Yesterday we navigated the heights, but today, as if he knows, the small man directs us steadfastly towards the coast. The first and even the second lap do no harm, but the third pass takes us dangerously close to a small yard, a corner of a field that seems to have been excerpted from the town, loosely visible now through the lifting fog. I shuffle a little in my steps, blinker my eyes. Progress back and forth is slow; the ground rising from the cliff gets steeper each round and we tire as the sun, now intermittently visible, approaches lunch. Some of us begin to look down, favouring angles of our boots, easy limping to offer preference to blisters. Others are aching in their hips, knees and shoulders; we have moved through the warming stage, where the pains lessen, into the weary throb of hours when grudges are reasserted and become compelling. My own have been sublimated into anxiety. For now. We turn at the bottom of a subsidiary rise and plod back towards the ocean.

The enclosed yard is directly in line with my steps. I can see the small cairn of stones marking your rest, Maree. Nubeena, the peninsula bloke, might catch the edge on the right, vault over and do the job. The others will miss it entirely. I approach the fence, lightly strung with bent wire snaking through fresh wooden posts, already wrinkling and warping in the moist air, and rest my hand against one, pausing as our grid search continues past me, a muddy rainbow out of sync. At the cliff's brim the small man is standing and watching.

'Thought so,' he says. He had swivelled immediately to see whether I would carry through. 'Come on, get over it. Get it done. Or else you're done too. Sure there's someone down there who could do proper work.'

The other men have twigged to the disturbance in the midst of their relief at finishing a stretch, their boredom at having to deal with another. I don't move. My hand still rests on the wood, one or two fingers leaning down to greet the wire.

'Need one of us to do your job for you?' He turns towards Howrah, who nods his head. He is a man who can get his hands dirty; he slopes over to the fence and climbs, swinging on the wire. I take three or four steps, grab hold of his shoulder and pull him off balance to the ground. He falls awkwardly, swears, gets up holding his back and spurs his other fist forward to grab me by the shirt. For a moment I think he will back off – the sores – but he is caught in a limbo between disgust and fury. The others look on, suddenly interested. The small man gestures to Kaoota, who is uncertain; is he being instructed to help Howrah pound me into the ground, or finish off the transect? The Lilliputian bows to the enclosure, but as Kaoota steps forward, I grab Howrah's wrist, twist it round till he is forced to bend to the ground, drop him flat and get up in Kaoota's face. He stops, checks back with the small man.

'Well.' The Lilliputian has his hands on his hips. 'Interesting, this. You want I just get everyone to pound seven shades out of you? You want to maybe slip sideways over there in a tragic bloody accident?' But his cockiness is wary; Howrah is lying on the ground holding his arm, and Kaoota is shuffling back and forth on the spot.

'Leave it,' I say. 'This yard stays.'

'What's that to you?' asks the small man. 'What you got in there? Buried your treasure? Pair of old dacks?' He spits out into space. I think of hurling him after his drool. He searches the eyes of the mainlanders but they have lowered their gaze; they are far from solid ground. 'Well, anyway, never should have got locals involved,' he says, trying to garner wisps of support. Kaoota backs off, pulls out a cigarette, and Howrah struggles up, carefully skirts an orbit around me and sits with the others near the spread of sky, the water crashing restlessly below. 'Some sort of revenge? Gonna wipe your rank face all over mine, give me a taste?' I continue staring at him. He snuffles, wipes his nose across a sodden sleeve. The birds idle backwards and forwards above the scene, uncertain of what this will spell.

We have been eradicating my islands. We carry map and compass; we expose the sea and annotate the charts.

It's true that I had hoped for certain memorial perks.

'You can take out the lot fading out down there round the hill,' I offer, pointing down to the edgelands bordering a few homes that are adrift from the dense cluster. 'Reckon a couple of weeks will see it through, then there's just the town and the port to rub. But you'll leave me the field.'

'Well,' says the Lilliputian, sensing wriggle room. 'See, I'm under contract. Eradication ain't complete unless it's full. Never know what could multiply from a little patch like that.'

'Your blokes I understand.' I gesture towards the mainlanders, scratching at my raw face. 'They've a job and they'll bugger off back to the mainland and dig spuds, send letters and get them. But you, what's happening to your island, I would have thought you might have wanted to get preserving.'

The Lilliputian looks livid for a moment, then draws on centuries of calm. The four Tasmanians are suddenly frightened; they don't want to get involved in whatever is going to happen next. 'Yeah,' says the Lilliputian, as they ease back from the edge. 'Go on, start a new sweep, be with you in a minute.' He watches them depart and waits till they are out of earshot.

'It's fucking different,' he says.

'Could be.' I shake my head wearily. 'Not different enough, though.'

We stand on the lip of land, the newborn escarpments that just last week were flowing fields sloping gently to a pebble beach, the town's cemetery sojourning on the fringes until we savaged them with our navigation, disappearing turf and blanking out the peat, felling the bridge that linked us to the bottom of the sea.

I take a few seconds to look around me, to breath it all in. I think there are birds flickering the air. I think there are rounded hills, shrubs gripping the dirt and stones that can be kicked. I think there is smoke rising from the mouths of the squat chimneys brewing in the homes that I think are in the valley below. The sky is there, the sky and the widening tumbledown sea. I think that the Lilliputian and I have hands, but I don't know what they will do.

But I think your mark will last much as others do, Maree.

All Hollows

The first door is split directly from the centre of a swamp gum and is blocking up its home, swaddled in the bush. The timber's grain ploughs its length and a fist of brass knocker presses its knuckles out of the wood. As I float down the sandstone path, dressed as a vampire, the eucalypts living in flower swirl all around me and their scent rains down and the sound of their smell is a bright and comforting chime of sweet wetness. And yet I am frightened – for a long time I've been unable to sleep. I've been wandering the evening lost, hunting for the wisdom of those who are said to walk this night, crowded and alone. Shocked possums crackle the bark; a car engine groans in the distance over a hill.

As I reach up and grip the knocker I feel both alive and dead. I lift it high like a swing and let it fall and the breeze rushes past its face, then it bellows in shock, startled by the door, its raw voice booming down the hallway and through the rooms of the house. A silence stretches out and then jagged shrieks slice at the night; the plovers have caught my smell. A clock is ticking in my head, the cadence echoed by a growing set of muffled steps. The lock relaxes, the door opens and an old, grey man with a flannel shirt flagging on his white skin stands expectant. 'Ah,' he says doubtfully, 'well, this year I'm prepared,' and he reaches back towards a wide glass bowl filled with spangled sweets that rustle in their nest as his hand disturbs their rest. 'Wait,' I say, 'I am searching for more a trick than treat – though the treat could be embedded in the trick.' His hand waits and it is dubious, so I hurry to explain all my driven wakefulness to the old man, how I lie in the dark and it bustles me with worries, how my brief dreams are trumpets blasting me awake, how my eyes are thinning and my mind flattening into two dimensions. I have tried powerful herbs and pharmaceuticals, I tell him. I have numbered threads of wool.

'I am knocking on your door,' I say to him. 'Do you remember your grandfather? My grandfather always talked about the war, but he never told me how to fall asleep. But perhaps our generations are bumpy and uneven; there might be those who have passed on secret stories, narratives that will carry us to rest. Can you help me with this trick?'

He continues to grasp and assess the chocolates as though they are what I truly want. 'Well,' he says. 'I can't say that I'm any sort of expert.' He scratches at his thinning hair. 'I've always thought about the gold nugget I'll stumble on in the Kennebec patch at the bottom of the yard. My name written on buildings and sails. These ambitions settle my evenings.'

As the old man speaks my heart groans, his narratives puff me up with the day; they yell at me and shake me and urge me to spring from my sheets and run up the hill and write letters to powerful patrons, for this man has no more wisdom to give me than the wallabies who flee down the unlit gravel roads. It is suddenly unclear to me if I waft forward, felling the slab door from his hands and its hinges, and reach for his neck, driving in my fangs and sucking at his life, his death, his waking and sleeping, or if I accept his proffered sweet – and then, as I stagger away in my cape, bent in weeping and frustration, I appear (from the perspective of a masked owl clouding the sky) to be a bat flying low against the ground.

2.

The second door is a steel screen mesh straining mosquitos and flies, and it fronts a clone-brick house on a patch of land varnished with dry and dying lawn. This grass stretches across the yard, over fruit trees and fences, across the clothesline with its singlets. It is beginning to threaten the house. The yard is bordered by a wall of bored aspidistras sitting on the edge of the street. They watch the pedestrians and the traffic; at any moment they could reach down and hurl a small stone through an open window. The wind follows behind me and the bushes avert their faces, for I am dressed as a werewolf and the burden of fur is hot on my skin; my claws are naked and sharp as they shred the dense night air.

I have been prowling through cemeteries tonight, hunting for a waltz with the bones of an emperor or slave, to whisper hopeless nothings in their skulls as they turn their own bared teeth to me and offer up the secrets of sleep. But the gravestones have all stood firm. There was no-one silhouetted in the churchyards, so I was forced to give them up and saunter through the suburbs to this house.

I pad up the firm grass path and rattle the door. It is not locked. 'Hello,' I call. 'Is anybody there?' I open it a crack. The hallway is paved with tired oak boards and a faded rug. There is a side table messed with papers, bills, and in the corner, an overflowing rubbish bin. A doorbell is nestled just outside the building; when I press it, a buzzer alarms the house. My ears stand tall and my eyes flicker left and right. There is a jumbling sound from a rear room, as though a bookcase has been overturned or a border collie has leapt among the garden furniture, then a door swings open and a middle-aged man staggers up the hallway with two children attached to one leg, half-dressed as soldiers or policemen. They turn their attention from the man's knee – it seems as though they want to reach out and stroke my coat. Instead they begin climbing up their father like a palm.

'Hi,' he manages, holding them off, 'nice costume.' He is probably thinking that I am a little old, but nonetheless he reaches for the rubbish bin and offers me, successively, an apple core, a broken plastic knife and an empty container of souring milk.

'Please,' I say. 'I don't want or need your treats so much as a trick; the truth is that I haven't slept in a long time.' And I describe the dread that hangs over every moment, drowning my clarity, and how I am certain that below this dread there is a true terror that seeps through my skin, for when I sit down at tables there are those who pack up their newspapers and move to another chair, and when I am walking down the street there are many who leap to the side and cover their faces as though I am spread with tumours and boils, as though I am coughing up illnesses. A strange beastliness has overtaken me – my eyes are wide as headlights, I am sullen and ill-humoured, I snap at simple comments and have lost the art of gentleness and consideration; but I am certain it would all be fixed if I could only get one night's sleep.

'So tell me,' I say, 'have you any stories left that might trick my system into letting go its hold?'

The man looks me in the eye, then he turns to his children and begins to cover their ears with his hands, and when he runs out of hands he pries the children from his leg and picks them up, one in each arm, and speaks to them and promises them picture books filled with lions and geese and ushers them through a nearby door and then returns to me, nearly whispering. 'Sex,' he says, 'although, that's not quite true. Not the thought of sex, but the expectation. I play out a scenario in my head. I drop in to my wife's best friend, offering a mattock I'd promised to lend or checking something about her kids; they are going to stay at our place on the weekend. And then we get to talking, and there is an excuse to touch a shoulder or a finger and then after that, well, I don't know. The conclusions are in dreams I can't remember; by then I've always drugged myself to sleep.' He shrugs and assumes a normal, louder, business-like tone, as though he is at my home and selling me tonics. 'It's always worked for me anyway,' he says, beginning to close the fly-screen door.

My mind is struggling from its well. I want to say that I have tried this story too, I have run this kind of film but it consumes me with guilt and despair and I am left more wakeful than before, needing to confess and beg forgiveness, and hunting out anything that resembles the light; so I lift my voice up to the moon and the stars and I howl, long and mournfully. In the flurry of confusion that follows I do not know if the screen door clangs against its frame as I turn and lope hopelessly back through the grass, silver threading my veins as I roam through distant hills, or if my howl becomes a roar as I leap forward and try to rip his throat from his neck until he fights me off screaming and runs for his bedroom or the door that guides me to the bedroom of his vulnerable children.

3.

The third door is open. It is wide, like a cave in the side of a concrete block at the end of a corridor at the summit of an elevator in a massive aggregation of apartments in the middle of a dingy and sparkling city. The light above my head is flickering as though it cannot decide on which side to fall. Ahead of me the apartment is laid out in bright metal and white, and nothing can settle on its surface, no virus, bacteria or dirt, no habits or foibles; it is like the glaze of a new frying pan that cannot grasp at an egg no matter how much it juggles, and I wonder if I will be able to balance on its polish, or if I will slip with my first step and slide all the way down the hall, out on to the balcony and into the smog-filled sky. I am not sure on my feet this evening – I have little grace or poise – I am dressed as a zombie, my clothes are torn, face bruised and bloody, and my eyes are hollow and bleached.

I lurch into the apartment, moaning. In the lounge there is a young man sitting precisely on a cream chair, his neat face in profile. He appears calm and alert. As I stumble down the hallway he slowly turns his head. 'Oh yes,' he says, 'I have something for you,' and he reaches down to a glass coffee table and retrieves a shotgun, glistening and brutal, and he pumps the action and points the gun towards me.

'Wait,' I say, 'I am not searching for a treat so much as a trick,' and I explain that for so long I have been lying down, unable to move, and when I do rise it is impossible to step with crispness or articulation; it is as though I am perpetually drunk, dropping mugs of coffee and running into telegraph poles, and even when I move with relative clarity I am completely unable to think. My brain has become barren, a desert, or the surface of the moon, or even the void of space through which the moon orbits, empty and freezing, and all through the hours of day and night I remain in the same state, as though my waking and resting have blended and combined in a single inhuman way of being. Yet I am sure these dreadful tendencies would reverse, if only I could find a story that would send me peacefully to sleep. And the young man, with the gun lowered slightly yet still firmly aimed in my direction, considers for a moment, shakes his head, and says, 'truthfully, I don't have a story for you. I've never found that I needed one. Wherever I am, sitting in a bus or jogging by the river, I can nod off and rest for as long as I like, and I'll always wake up exactly when I need to. In fact, I was sleeping in this chair while you floundered your way down the corridor, but as soon as you trespassed into my flat I was perfectly awake.'

At this my head sinks, for this man can be of no help to me. And so perhaps I accept his generous treat; perhaps I blunder towards him with my stiff arms raised and he lifts the gun and fires, again and again, and the sound fills the crisp apartment like the silence that follows, and I fall on his spotless rug, and as I keep my blood to myself, perhaps I find the depths for which I've been longing, drifting into peace, joining the quiet ghosts waiting on the other side. But it could also be that even here I have been utterly tricked and there is no sleep, no rest, nothing that can swell me into safety; no-one, anywhere, who will set me apart in their thoughts and call out prayers for my soul.

The Slide

1.

Julie Rose has the longest slide in the world.

The theme park people sweat in queues outside her door, counting the bricks in the footpath as the doorbell echoes through the hallways. Sometimes Julie shoos them away; more often she asks me to do it while she strolls over to the slide. Every theme park wants the slide as a featured attraction, and their people offer ridiculous sums of money, but they really want the slide for themselves. They'll slip away to the South Pacific as soon as the contract has been signed. Julie knows this because I told her. 'Don't trust them,' I yelled behind me as we rode down the slide one windy afternoon. 'Those fucks will be away with this slippery beauty.' Julie had reached for the edges to sense the warmth of nearly-friction beneath her hands; the burning air hurtling as though she was cupping a plasma ball just about ready to burst.

I also want the slide.

When I saw it standing in her yard like a towering fast food pillar, I began following Julie to her work at the primary school. I chanced upon her in the pub. We sat next to each other at the bar and when she ordered her drink, I turned to her and complimented her vowels.

Her eyebrows got caught up in her hair.

'Your vowels,' I repeated. 'They're stunning. Could you say "beer"?'

Elocution. Try it. Years ago, my friend Kevin and I split over consonants and vowels, but vowels have always been triumphant.

'Beer?' said Julie with an upturned note in her voice like she was asking a question, pouring the rising tones into the space between us.

'Beautiful,' I said. 'Yes, of course.'

Soon I was sleeping at her place. Every morning we got up early and shot down the slide.

2.

The slide takes a full five minutes. You could start poaching an egg at the top and it would be overdone by the time your feet slapped the pinebark. You could recite 'The Rime of the Ancient Mariner' if you spoke quickly and skipped over the slow bits. You could clean out your microwave, consolidate your super funds, see an osteopath. Julie and I have done all of these things and more.

'How does it work?' she is asked.

It is in a small suburban block. There are roses, a birdbath. A canape yard offering titbits of flower and stem. The jealous kids next door watch grimly, barely bouncing on their thinning, unprotected trampoline.

'Why don't you invite them over?' I once suggested.

'They throw rocks,' Julie replied, 'at cats.'

Julie loves animals. She is always picking up small dogs and insects and giving them a turn on the slide.

'Could *you* throw rocks at cats?' she asks.

I think back to rocks and cats.

'No,' I say. 'Of course not.'

3.

The theme park people keep coming. Kevin is the most persistent.

'Fuck off Kevin,' I yell when he bothers the door with his briefcase. 'We don't want you here.'

'Barney,' he says calmly, 'we both know it's not your slide. It's Julie's. So why don't you let me speak to her?'

Kevin and I used to play *Call of Duty* after school. Now we blank each other in the street and only speak at Julie's door. I look across at her, peeking from behind a curtain. She shakes her head. 'Julie doesn't want to speak to you just now,' I say. 'She's getting sick of you hassling her.'

'I can see you, Julie!' says Kevin, looking at the other window. 'I know you're there. Anytime you want to talk, you've got my number.' He turns and walks back down the path, nods to the queue of theme park guys at the gate, standing there like a series of princes who have failed in their quests.

4.

I don't like to say that the slide will be mine, but the slide will be mine. Where I grew up in the poorer suburbs, nobody made much of an effort with parks. A square of grass, a fence and a sign – we rode around on our bikes, splashing up mud and skidding. That was it. Where were the swings?

Where was the slide?

The first slide I remember was in a park near the centre of the city. We were there for something dental and afterwards I couldn't talk, so Dad took me there to make up for it all. I stood at the top of its beautiful red spiral. It seemed fast and certain. A girl half my size in a blue hoodie squeezed in beside me.

'Well, are you going to go?' she asked.

I couldn't say anything.

'Do you mind if I go?' she asked.

Still, I couldn't speak.

Later, I gritted my numb teeth and slid down the curves, but by then the girl had gone and my Dad was sitting on a bench staring at joggers.

5.

Julie trusts me. This is a good thing. But I have to wait till she leaves me alone with the slide. It's not a matter of twenty minutes to pack it in its case and heave it into the back of the car. Plus there are the theme park people. Once, Julie asked me to tighten a bolt in the cork-screw section. There was pandemonium outside. Kevin was shouting at the top of his lungs. 'Julie! Wrench! Barney's got a wrench!' I climbed the ladder, slid down to the offending bolt and tightened it, very slowly, while staring them down. The street chorus grew quiet. I gave it one final tighten and then slid down the rest of the slide, staring, as they came into view around each corner. At the bottom, I tossed the wrench near the fuchsias and strolled inside. A good dry run. The chance will come.

It's helpful that Julie and I spend so little time together. She goes off to teach at school, I head to the office. After work, I catch the bus and then wait on the porch till she gets home to unlock the door. One day she will forget and this will be my chance. One night she will sleep soundly and neglect to turn off the alarm. One day there will be a perfect chance to get her and the others away from the house.

A party. I will throw a party in honour of Julie and the slide and invite all the theme park people.

6.

'How lovely!' says Julie. 'You're so kind, Barney.'

'Well Julie,' I say. 'I loooooveee youuuu.' I really let my vowels show.

'What are you up to?' asks Kevin at the gate, fingering his invitation as I head out to buy balloons and streamers and hundreds and thousands for fairy bread.

'A party,' I say. 'I'm up to a party. Are you coming? Or don't you care about Julie?'

'Oh, I'm coming,' he says, shoving the invitation back into his pocket.

7.

You can see the slide from space. You can see it from the moon. The slide makes its presence felt in weather patterns. Scientists can detect gravity waves from the slide. Free-climbers have failed to summit the slide. There are rainbows; we swoosh through them and feel their reds, yellows and greens against our faces. We are constantly refusing tower requests from broadcasters and mobile phone companies. Flight-paths have changed. Sometimes there is snow at the top of the slide. The slide contains rare minerals and we stand at the bottom when it is raining to filter them from the pouring stream. The slide makes me laugh. The slide makes me cry. The slide reaches up to heaven.

They built a huge slide over at BigWorld™ but it was nowhere near the size of Julie's. The designers were fired and they got new design-ers to try to stretch it out. Not even close.

The slide is getting bigger; now it takes a good twelve minutes. Soon, we'll be able to slide all day and it will be the same as having the slide for myself.

It will not be the same as having the slide for myself.

I proceed with my plans.

8.

We hold the party upstairs at the local pub. I make sure there are banners. 'Hooray for Julie! And Also for the Slide!' The balloons and streamers look wonderful. Someone has brought a Christmas tree, which feels incongruous, and I see Kevin sniggering. He looks at me across the table, lifts a slice of fairy bread to his mouth. Winks.

We do the speeches early so that everyone can get smashed. I stand before the crowd, explaining how wonderful Julie is, and how much we enjoy riding on the slide. Everyone claps a little bit. Julie says how grateful she is for the party, that she is always surprised by how much everyone loves the slide, but that she loves the slide too, so perhaps she isn't really that surprised. She sits down as everyone cheers and whistles, then stands up again. 'Oh yes, and thanks Barney.'

One of the theme park people stands up, pulls a few notes from his pocket. He coughs. Everyone refills their glasses for the toasts, and then they just refill their glasses. Julie is over the other side of the room whispering to Kevin.

This is my chance.

I hurry out the door, run down the street and leap the fence into Julie's yard, where I hunt down the wrench by the fuschias. The slide is like a mountain rising up above me. I climb the ladder – the slide has to be dismantled from above – and sit at the top, staring at the view across the suburbs, the town, the fields, farms and other mountains rubbing up against the sky. Then I reach for the first bolt and start to twist it. The wrench is heavy in my hand. I loosen the bolt, take it out, hold it in my palm. It is grey like a cloud. I put it in my pocket, take it out again.

What am I going to do with this bolt?

I put it back in its slot and tighten it.

For a long time I sit with the view, but when I finally push off, watching as the stars swirl down like the storming rain, I think of Julie, the way her hair rushes behind her, at the way she laughs at my excellent jokes. I feel a bit sorry. Maybe we could run away to the South Pacific or something; sit on the beaches, drink cocktails and slide all the way from volcanic heights into clear blue water. We could take time to cuddle in bed and then slide all day till we are weary with climbing. I could propose! Now I wish that I had brought the bolt with me. On the way down, I could have shaped it into a ring.

Finally, the slide peters out. At the bottom, Julie is standing with Kevin.

'Got a report about a loose bolt,' I say, showing them the wrench.

'All fixed. How's the party going?'

Julie breathes in. 'Barney,' she says, 'You're going to have to collect your things.'

'What?' I say.

The wrench slips from my fingers.

'You're going to have to collect your things.'

Kevin looks triumphant.

'What do you mean?' I ask.

'Kevin is going to be staying with me for a while. There won't be room for you both. You're going to have to go.'

'Yeah, fuck off Barney,' says Kevin.

'But why?' I ask as the tears glisten in my eyes.

There is a silence.

It feels like something has begun sliding from a great height all the way down to the lowest depths.

I can't speak.

'Oh Barney,' says Julie. 'He loves my 'b's. He loves my 'c's and 'd's! He even loves my 'k's. Especially when I say his name.'

Atlantis Minor

'Crotty is back on the map, thanks to one of the driest
summers on record... The ruins of the once thriving mining town
are soaking up sunlight because of the shrinking Lake Burbury,
just one of many hydro lakes that are at historically low levels.'
The Saturday Mercury, February 14th 2016.

'Crotty!' I yelled. 'It's back!' Rushing home, I started heaving raw
supplies in to the back of the car while Suzy hugged her belly in the
driveway. For here was Crotty risen – it was risen indeed! – and even
though we had never lived in this town, never seen its ruin slumped
in the valley's rest, scratching its head and trying to push through the
scrub of dementia to its mining past, we knew that we had hung our
shirts on its lines, slept in its beds, sculled beers in its pub past the
hours of closing, that we had played for its footy team and pruned its
apple trees, that we had shivered by its fires and argued in its kitchens,
that we had punched through its midnights and sulked in its sheds.

In the city I was feeling swamped like a grey, once-living tree with
its crown spiderwebbing from the water. Pushing around words and
scrunching their pages into clusters of static. On weekends I had
been flattening my body against maps, dreaming up the streets of
old towns and smelling their gardens in the paper's ink. These towns
had been torn from the charts and glued into history books, mining
towns that had been scrubbed from the world and lived on, unbus-
tling, in text; abstracted homes settling down in suburbs of paper.
Town as typescript: helvetica homes. Town as form: platonic streets.
Black and white images of men and women in loose clothes leaking
the years. All that enterprise and hope packed up into such thin cases,
unpacked in two dimensions.

But there we stood at the edge of the dry impoundment like so many bold settlers, thanking the cable for its fraying and failure, thanking the sun and all the blue depths for the long, dry summer, the summer that had dwindled the lake and carried off our power to the sea. And even though we knew that as winter came on, thousands of poor and elderly people would be shivering in their cardboard homes as their lights clocked off and the bars of their heaters shame-lessly unblushed; that as forgetfulness swept over laptops and phones, as ovens yawned and went to sleep, yes, there would be people who would die from the cold. The last few drops of water would drib-ble through the turbines like loose bronze coins from empty pockets, our sickly island economy going down for the third time in a dry pool; the tills silent, the smelters tipping all that ore back into sea. The island sinking or drifting even further from the mainland than it had managed. There would be nowhere to buy bread. The wheat in the fields would reach up to tickle our fringes and the newspapers would be blank. The sound of private diesel generators would echo in the valleys, the tourists would visit Syria and Yemen before they would think to spend bristling dollars in our shut-down state.

But we would not care. For we would have this town.

Crotty: not a prepossessing name. You would not die for Crotty or bundle your body into a ship and sail across the ocean. You would not sell Crotty to an investor speculating on whims.

And yet *viva* Crotty! Crotty died, but long may Crotty live!

What had we to lose? With the power choked we would all be living in darkness soon enough; and here was this restored glow out west. So holding hands, we slid across the silt, our sneakers bruised with dirt and our shoulders weighed down with so much settling. Leading couples picked through the foundations, searching out those that best suited them among the low, rectangular piles of bricks. Perhaps this was not such a clear footing to straddle a dream across, but our eyes were glazed with excitement and we launched our tents over those forgotten homes and then as the evening shadowed us with dark green hills, we gathered as one in the ruins of the old church and gave thanks for this resurrection.

In the morning we woke to the sound of trickling water. Heads turtled out of tents and inspected the streets. They were dry. Were the echoes of the lake so dense that they were still rebounding off the ruins? We shook our heads and laughed, emerging into another clear-hearted day. One man, a friend I had known in another life, crouched down outside his home and lit up an old gas choofa stove. The sweetness of boiling oats tickled our noses. We slipped down to what remained of the lake and kicked it in the guts, dragging a few more billies from its thirst. We gathered softer branches and leant against them as the tea met tannin and boiled into bitterness.

'Friends!'

We looked up from our bustling stoves.

The words boomed from the man who had been stewing oats. He was standing on a broken slab of concrete, almost completely still; a man on the path to statuedom. The tea smouldered in our palms and we shuffled up around him, a group of twenty, thirty pioneers with red flannel shirts, torn jeans and thermals on our skin.

'Friends,' he repeated, 'this is a great day! For nearly thirty years this town has been lost to us, buried beneath the lake, but now it has emerged.' And so it had, the drained streets and all its finned citizens bailing or bailed into the diminishing puddles tickling the dam's feet. 'And this,' he continued, 'this town has been like a lost relative we never had the chance to meet. But look, the graves have been upended! Our histories are flesh!'

He reached down to a patch of dark mud and planted a seed. A single rolled oat that would never grow, an oat with all the potential squeezed out of it long ago; but as a symbol this seed sent a green shoot plunging through our imaginations. We would grow crops here, we would settle down far from the cities in this almost-myth, and nothing that had been lost to us could hurt us again. Our families, our weatherboard homes and the years marching past would all be returned to us. A cheer went up as he smoothed the dirt across that lifeless seed, a round of applause, and all that rallying sound was like the chattering of a rocky stream, a busy, energetic rivulet. Nervous for a moment, I looked around at the flushed faces, and then joined in the celebration with even more gusto.

As we dispersed through the earthy streets, Suzy and I thought to plant something of ourselves in the soil as a ritual of sacrifice and thanksgiving.

'What do you want to plant?' she asked. And she looked a little sad and hungry, and I remembered again how she had been resistant to coming out here on the day that we heard the news. 'We have a home,' Suzy had said, 'we're having a child. Anyway, they're going to get the power back on some time.'

But now here she was, asking this most pressing of questions.

'My hand,' I was about to answer. 'I was thinking of planting my right hand.' But I saw her interest tighten into concern as a gurgle rolled beneath us. This time we did not rush outside, but sat thoughtfully in our new home, eying the cut-off fireplace and wavering walls, the mats stretched out on the floor with mildew clinging to their sides, the sweaty sleeping bags and chaos of food and clothing. The gusting mosquitoes who came and plundered, the dozens of flies and mosquitoes who trembled the air with a constant buzz like heavy rain pounding on the blue tarp roof.

And it seemed, as we sat there, that the space in our murky home filled up with those grim, lifeless insects so that we couldn't see the walls, the roof or each other, a dense fog that blocked out the room and trickled out into the town, cluttering the sky with slabs of cloud, and when we ran out into the blurred streets and stood there alone in that abandoned town heavy with thick grey air – as we lunged around and searched through the pattering ruins – the tears began raining down my face.

'Where did you go?' I shouted as we pounded through the lost, deserted streets. 'Where did everybody go?'

Below Tree Level

Dirt leaves dissolved in water, invisible sediment flavouring the snow. Drops so dense with minerals that the weak sun glints fiercely off the surface of the creek. I don't know whether the water is healthy or flowering cancers in my intestines, but with every coffee I'm feeling heavier, as though I'm being poured downstream and sinking into the estuary's silt.

It's been five days of mornings where the sun moves as slowly as a calendar. Sitting by the waking fire, coaxing it into life, praising the small steps as it comprehends and catches the thinner twigs; adding branches, testing its strength as it comes into its own. This morning it sparks at the influx of air, cheered at the prospect of company. I rest the billy on the flames and stir the dried coffee in my cup, as though it's already brewing. This is my hopeful moment of the day. Later in the evening I'll go to bed knowing there's something to look forward to.

I take hold of a branch, ground down by coals, and stoke the flames. The sparks brighten the hut for a few brief seconds and I feel myself reflected; fingers knotted in greasy hair, and stiff clothing that coats my body like a shell. Over the past week, I've become more dirt and the hut has become more me. Given time, I'm sure we'll rot into each other like a married couple.

The image brings to mind my brother and his wife. Seeing one without the other, sitting at the bus stop or waiting in a queue at the supermarket, they look as though they're prematurely grieving. When Mike dropped around the other day it was the first time he'd visited alone in over a year.

I'd been disoriented by my first week of holidays, overwhelmed by the space in my mornings and afternoons. My sleeping pattern was established and it would have been easier to change address than doze the morning away. Coffee on the machine at home, check the email, some shopping. Sitting in the sun with a breezy paper. Daytime television. A sense of being planted on my couch and forgetting exactly who I was, what I was meant to be doing. Mike had knocked on the door. He had stood there, carefully watching a passing car before turning to meet my eyes.

We'd carried toasted sandwiches outside and sat on cushions on the small concrete balcony that doubled as a path reaching across my front door.

'Why don't you head up to the bush? You've been wanting to for years. Retreat. Re-evaluate.'

'There are only so many days of leave. I want to use them properly.'

'So get around the forest. You know what the forest does for me.'

'Not sure if I should get a project, build something. Build a wall.'

'A real experience of nature. Let it open your eyes and clear out your head.'

'It would just be digging a hole in reverse. Why do I want to dig a hole? Why do I want to build a wall?' I wiped my hands under the cushion and finished them on my trousers. Mike shrugged and pulled a jumper over his head.

Three long days filled with thin light in the streets and dense, flat shade in my room. My mind was full of oily hands that couldn't grip anything for more than a moment. I walked from room to room, pulled books off the shelves and returned them. I stared out the window at the fish and chip shop across the road and thought about buying something to eat or making something to eat. I watched people walking and noticed the way the wind seemed to animate their hair and clothes as leaves were tossed around them, catching in trees. I thought about what Mike had said and reached into the wardrobe for my pack. I knew where I was going, or a part of my brain knew and it was directing my actions.

Someone remembers thirteen guideposts from the turnoff, someone else thirty-one. There are dirt runs resembling the beginning of tracks at both. Most of the huts in the forests aren't marked on maps; you have to know where to go. Dad had spoken about this one when we were kids, though I'm not sure if he'd ever been here. He showed me photographs – no, they were slides – of weekends he'd spent in mountain cabins, splashing in pools and cooking toast over the fire. I'd assumed this was one of them but now that I'm up here, it doesn't look like those images projected by the slides, which were full of light no matter how gloomy the environment. Having followed what I remembered of his route, I'm starting to wonder if there are huts everywhere, a whole city of cabins at the end of every track.

This hut is built into the rock like fungus crouched on a stump; leaning back, every plank resting with its feet up. Stone steps sink into the clay soil beside an empty box for firewood. There's a window near the apex that lights the moisture coating the walls. Inside, the hut is a fallen trunk, dark and irregular, built around and focused on the fire that is slowly carrying my billy to boiling. I stare at the mountain water, sweating the pot and breathing steam. I'd carried water in, the plastic water assembled in factories, but I dribbled it away when the creek first called to me around the corner of the track. As if the rainforest was parched and my act of mercy would trickle across its tongue and bring colour to its cheeks. In reality the forest is flooded, fat with moisture and ready to burst. Fog thickens the air and insects crumple logs the size of dinosaur bones.

The billy has boiled and I realise I've poured my coffee and started drinking. I look around, expecting something to have changed, some movement of the bunks or scratchings on the walls, but every slab of wood is set in place and the dust is steady in the cracks. I wait a little longer, sipping the coffee and hoping the caffeine is keening my senses. My shoe scratches against the floor and it conjures the sound of leather on stone.

The door tries to open but catches on the warped frame. Another tug shudders it free and an older woman appears. Her figure forms a weak silhouette that reveals her colours and folds. Late fifties or sixties, hair twisting around her face. She shrugs her pack on the other bunk and her boots test the floor for hollowness. Unburdened, she returns to the open door to breathe, it seems, for she takes several large lungfuls of air and pours them back into the atmosphere. Staring out at the leafy masses as though about to make a speech. I wait for her to begin talking, to me at least if not the forest, but she is silent and seems content to remain so.

I add some wood to the fire and the flames slump, disenchanted. It's not good wood. Partly decomposed, it was resting peacefully in its grave when I robbed it, too lazy to walk the extra few metres to find strong-boned branches. The first day I wandered along the track for about ten minutes, but it started angling downhill and I didn't want a long walk later in the afternoon. Since then I've kept to smaller and smaller circles around the hut as though focusing in on a target.

I turn from the wheezing fire and see that the woman has left the hut. I get up and walk over, expecting to see her drinking at the creek or sitting on a rock inspecting her boots, but she's already out of sight, up or down the track. I look back at the bunk to make sure her pack is real. It sits alert on the edge of the bed, ready to leap off and tramp up a hill to find a waterfall. My gaze flicks to the forest. On rare days the sun slashes scars against the floor, just enough to provide a hint of warmth, but today it has been clouding over and the breeze has been wringing the heat from the day. The hills across the valley look mournful and I can understand if they are despairing. On days like these I can imagine the trees retracting into the ground to hibernate.

When I first arrived I spent more than an hour sitting on a rock, just staring at a collection of undertrees. My eyes were fixed as if a storyline was being unveiled before me, and I was a part of that storyline. They seemed filled with energy. I was sure they walked to the gully to drink from the stream in the evening and that their fallen companions got up in the morning to stretch.

A little longer, and the trees began to shrink into their trunks. Over time they grew smaller still, matchsticks sticking out of the ground, a model maker's rejects on the side of the hill furthest from the train. I began to feel hungry and cold. I took my walk down the hill. I sat down by the fire. I didn't move for the rest of the afternoon and I've barely moved since.

The same trees stare at me now as I stand in the doorway. I'm about to resume my position by the flames when something grasps my attention. They seem particularly bent, older somehow, like they've seen more of life. They're huddled together and whispering. My eyes track along a branch and leap off, detour along the earth behind a small rise. A line of dirt appears gradually, slowly being drawn, and the picture opens up as I cross the space settled by the track.

A plot of ground has been flattened to clay. I walk around it without much interest. It's roughly square and doesn't look dug, more like a great foot had stamped it down overnight. Perhaps the wallabies are evolving. I like the thought of wallabies digging for native vegetables and decide that this is what I will believe the patch of ground is. I return to the hut, tempted to give the woman's bag a kick, or throw it into the bushes. I take my seat by the fire and poke the coals with my branch.

Though the mornings in the cabin are slow they do at least have a structure to them. The afternoons are more difficult to fill convincingly. I wait as long as possible for lunch. When there is only water in my veins and my head has become transparent I tear a packet of pasta open and throw it into the billy. I used milk for the first few days but the pasta seems to taste fine with just water. Afterwards, I fill the dirty pot and let it soak a few hours near the door. It sits there and doesn't quite freeze and I suppose it might be easier to clean when I'm ready to cook tea.

I brought a spiral bound notebook to serve as a logbook in the event the cabin didn't have one. I put my feet up and write a little. So far, looking back, my entries have been almost identical and I feel like I'm on a long sea voyage. I try to sleep, get up and move around the hut, count planks and cracks in the wood. I play with the fire, building bridges and burning them down. One thing to be grateful for at this time of year is the early dark. I can let myself believe it is later than it is. I get tired sooner anyway, as though the dark is more present and active on the parts of my brain that allow me to rest. Dinner is by candlelight; packet rice this time, with freeze-dried peas and carrots.

At the end of my meal I drift towards my sleeping bag. I try to settle down but my mind is occupied with my new companion. She has been hiding behind my thinking all afternoon and now that I've given up diverting myself I'm left with her presence. Is she from the city, like me, or does she live nearby in one of the tiny communities or fringe houses that sit in their shelves around the park borders? I wonder where she has gone and find myself concerned about her wandering alone all night. It's unreasonable to expect her to call in like a teenage daughter but this is the bush and things can happen. I lie back in my sleeping bag and think of her caught in a tree after stumbling off a blind ledge, tangled and broken. I twist myself tighter in my cocoon, and in time my conscience curls up and begins to doze and I wrap my arms around it.

I wake the next morning to the sound of metal and wood bathing together. The blur blinks from my eyes as I lift my head over the ridgeline of the sleeping bag. The fire is going and a hand moves away from a billy – my billy? – that is sitting in the burning wood. The woman is established on the bench, her woollen jumper stretched across her back, her hair falling behind like roots reaching for underground moisture. I want to ask her about the billy but her back is a wall and I can't imagine my voice carrying through it. I lean my head against my roughly folded jumper.

The woman has stolen my morning.

I try to go back to sleep, but her movements scatter sound around the cabin. Things are unwrapped and cut, boiled and poured. Her sipping is the kind that rattles a cup of tea, shakes it and interrogates it, then shouts it down your throat. The bench creaks as it adjusts to her shifting weight.

I am naked in my sleeping bag and feel uncomfortable about moving or even getting dressed within its boundaries. I decide to risk it, as even with her ritual movements there is something immobile about her. I swing the end of my bag off the bunk to the floor and dig my shirt out of the pile. Pulling it over my head, I push the sleeping bag off and drag my trousers on a little faster than normal. The woman doesn't turn.

As I pull on my shoes I feel divided. At one level I feel almost desperate to say something. This woman clearly knows the bush. She could suggest a walk. We could talk, have a normal conversation about the weather. Would she reply to rumours of clouds? Would she say anything at all? But she should have said something yesterday. It would have been polite to ask about sharing the hut. Instead, she stomped in and subdivided my space, reducing me to living on the tiny block of my bunk. I can't bring myself to say anything to this woman. Leaving the hut, I quietly pull the door to and walk towards the water without my billy.

It's a day where clouds are driven streakily across the sky; the sun kisses my face shyly before hiding behind them. The wind must be higher – although the air is bone cold, it's stationary and waiting. My sneakers, which haven't had a chance to warm after sleeping coverless through the night, are stung by ice crystals dying below them. I splash water across my face but it fails to freshen my feelings. I'd like, just once, to see a fish in the creek. It seems to be running slower, more languorously, and I put my hand in the flow and feel its gentle pressure before the chill forces me to retract it.

On the way back to bed I stop and have a piss, focusing on the small patch of frozen mud paralysed below me. I shake myself and think of looking at the cleared patch of dirt. I don't know if I'm expecting an apple tree or a crop of wheat, but it's clear something has grown overnight.

Below me the foothills of a hut have germinated and sprouted and begun reaching for the light. The back wall is filled with stones climbing over each other while the two sides are framed with wooden limbs and unevenly stepped logs. There is no front wall and the floor is the same pressed dirt as the previous day. It's not fully built, but it's no ruin either and my mind stumbles, trying to understand how someone could have made such progress, so silently on a dark, freezing night. I look back at my hut and think of the woman. Perhaps she was working on sections further from the site and dragged them together somehow? But why would she want another hut when she seems so satisfied taking mine?

I walk quickly to the hut and throw open the door. Her possessions, once ordered in her pack, have spilled and flowed over the floor, on to the bench, even lapping at my bunk. The fire has been reduced to coals and the woman has gone. I jump into my sleeping bag and huddle in a corner; the textures of damp wood read my back. I shut my eyes and open them again and think about packing up my things and leaving, going back to the city and my warm flat. The fire has gone to ashes so quickly. I wind myself tighter in my bag, trying to isolate myself from the world of ferns settling in valleys, aching air and melting wood.

For a moment I'm alone, lying in my bunk. The fire is gone, the morning is beginning again and my dreams are threads of screen on which a film is partially projected. The air is solid and it will be another few minutes before I can convince myself to push the sleeping bag away, jump into my clothes and begin my daily conversation with the fire. My trip to the stream for the water, my morning coffee ditching sleep and bringing my senses to bear on the day before me. I know that I'm in bed in my hut, and also that I'm about to emerge into a filthy, freezing hovel I'm thoroughly tired of and ready to escape. I'm in both of these places, yet the footsteps clearing a throat outside remind me I'm in another one, still, that is less and less mine to possess and enjoy.

'Well, I'm all for following on.' The woman's voice is lighter than I'd imagined. Is she talking to me or someone else? I wait for a moment. There is no answer, so I hesitantly call out.

'I just want my hut back.'

I'm aware of a headache drifting through my mind. A few seconds pass before she answers. 'How do you think we should do it?'

'I want my fire and my billy, I want to be able to sleep without worry. I want to wake and sleep knowing where I am.'

'Have you built the foundations?'

I'm still not certain that she is talking to me, so I stand from my bunk and throw open the door in time to see a pair of gaiters and boots disappearing down the trail leading from the hut. I run down the steps and try to catch her. The corners rush towards me and my knees hurt as I jolt around them, arms circling trees to loop around the bends. I come out into a straighter section and there is no sign of the woman. Thinking of my hut, overtaken and consumed, I'm suddenly panicked by the terror that if I leave it for any length of time her weeds will strangle me completely. Maybe she's already doubled back and all I'll find after gasping up the slope will be a hut choked with older woman. I'm torn between following her down the hill and losing myself entirely, but fear outpaces my curiosity and I start back up around the corners that hide the clearing. The clouds have filled out and the ground cover is shaded as though the canopy is growing thicker, and I seem to be pushing though the forest itself. The undergrowth makes my steps invisible and my body falls and jars itself in the hollows and rises. My trousers are wet and the hems have filled with mud. I slip against logs and the moss rubs off like a wound. I run up patches of scree that offer giant rock paths through the forest. All the trees are growing into each other, tiny fingers collected in a pack and great giants sitting on ledges, upright and legs crossed, branches fallen like disembodied limbs. The cold has become just cool, a cool the forest seems permanently set to throughout the year. There is wind in the trees now, or is it a waterfall, or is it huge brushing footsteps washing through the pandani behind me?

I begin a tripping run, crashing into saplings that shiver at my contact, feet that try to send me cartwheeling into the bushes. In a strange moment I'm aware that the forest isn't even green, it's all a blank, dull grey, layers of concrete and metal twisting and falling, colour leaching into the ground, ready to spring up again when the weather warms. I'm surrounded by mud ground and an iron roof and bars that reach higher than dozens of clambering arms.

I break into open space. Up ahead and to the side there is a massive tree carcass with a great root system splayed like welcoming arms. Ferns grow from the roof beside rocks clutched firmly. There is a tree cave growing with tiny root stalactites and I hurry through the embrace formed by the entrance and sit breathing heavily on the edge of a root or a rock. The quiet seeps through the leaves again and I feel the walls of my tree shifting gently, adjusting to my presence, and I'm not sure where I am or if it is safe but I know that I'm sitting in some sort of shelter and the misted rain that has started to fall is only making it stronger as it soaks the undergrowth above me.

Though it is light outside I find myself lying down below my roots, eyes closing, almost asleep in my tree cave. Moss settles around my neck and meets the curves, gently sponging away the dirt. It is quiet. There are no birds in this part of the forest and the drizzle is too light to quiver the ground. There is twitching in my nose with the fruiting of tiny spores of fungus. Insects crawl across my leg and grains of dirt rise from the ground and brush my skin. I'm kept on the edge of wakefulness only by the knowledge that someone else has entered the tree and has sat down by my feet; it is a body or it is nobody and she is making no sound. I cannot hear or smell her but I know she must be breathing.

Beast Evolving

'Can we keep him?' I asked. 'Look at him run!'

He was bounding up the hills, fetching sticks to burn and lapping up pools of water in grass and trees, in the bodies of possums and roos. Here in the city, we'd never had a pet like this – dogs who rained their skittering claws on the bones of old brick yard, cats that ladled their bodies into the hollows of our arms. Fish that circled the dead-dry pond like orange lights telling us to wait and watch; to follow them slow before they blinked behind a rock. But we hurried past their brief lives, struggled with their names – which cat had brown ears? Did he run away to feral hills on the eastern shore? Was he taken in the night or taken in the day? Was it just a long, slim needle that found its way precisely to a vein that made him just a little quieter than he'd been?

'Can we keep him?'

It would be fine: we would be cosy when the frost found fame in the depths of June. We brought him home and locked him in a box, dark like the metal had charred; in the early mornings and fading afternoons we would bolt him in that cell to heat our homes, and all his smoke would cough up the flue and smear the sky. We would pull a couch near and watch his tricks – dancing in the corner and begging for kindling – and in the night he would curl low around a couple of split logs: dense, hard cushions that yielded to his press and powdered to ash. Later we would sic him on the waste wood pruned from withering apples and plums that the new flies had fleeced; push him under a plate to sear the rare meat in the back end of swollen summers, seasons overweight and straining, sun fed, guts spilling into spring and autumn.

'Can we keep him?'

The bugger is he's always getting out, leaping through the door and hurtling through the gate when the kids have left it swung, running over cars and snapping at feathers and fur, scraping back the peat with coal claws and plucking so much pine in bright bouquets of flame. We watch in booing crowds as he's handed gum to gum, kicked long to the homes strung out drying in long lines of road, tackling their roofs and blistering the paint. Sure of his heft, measuring his height against the baking years graphed out in anxious charts, a beast evolving proud and strong – chest straining as his muscles flare – he grins a foul grin as he licks up leaves.

'Can we keep him?'

We try to put him down, splash water in his face to make him sleep; he gets up and snarls. We bury him in the yard, dig a kiln of clay to trap him as he fires, but he shatters the ceramic walls and races for the fence palings. We plug him up with drugs and knives, a new asbestos coat; he births huge litters and spreads his sparks across the state.

'Can we keep him?'

Here the footpaths are melting like old frost and the lawns have given up green; kids splash in dust and we water the tomatoes with drips of old sweat. Our city is a boiled egg with concrete cracks, and one tap can shatter the thinning shell. We take to the river for the miracle of fish; some set up home in its moat. Every winter we burn down the mountain and hope it will be enough. The harbour's wider now but its hands stop nothing till the flames have bulled our china shop of homes and gardens. We remember the years that suburbs were clear-felled and gingerly rebuilt – there are signs, commemorations to old Lenah Valley, Sandy Bay – thin regeneration. We don't get so attached. Parts of the city phoenix each year and we get to know the new bird rising as it learns the words and speaks to us anew: 'hello cocky, hope you like it here!'

The whole city: our hearth and home. We dress in threads of fear like we're being hunted: our lion cub that played and leapt and scratched us just a little has grown up and gone bush, gone wild. He's bred in there and he's coming back, and back, and the smoke is a blanket of new clouds forming shapes that none of us want to see, clouds that send the sun's eye red and weeping, clouds that make our own eyes feel like gravel roads, clouds that paint the borders of our lungs, that leave us hunting for our homes and the track to safety, for our mothers, fathers and children lost in all that brown, all that white, lost in the bodies of cremated trees sent high; our heavens damned with the cyclone of seasons picking up speed, whirring weather leaving us on the bare beach gasping.

'Can we keep him?'

We heard that years ago the fires danced in tight squares, hemmed in by the patterns of roads, old burns and the rhythmic rain that hammered their coffin lid down every season as the days closed in and the winds from the south flexed. This may have been a lie, some golden age tale when no gold flickered in the hills, when the wet came steady and long like a novel we read all year. Was this real or just a story? Maybe these were tree myths told in pages from their guts; maybe they were our myths, fictions we blew across the forests and forgot. Was there ever a time when half the year matched the other, when we didn't cower under a blunt threat that waited for the wind, the jagged spark in the sky, an angry god that called for flesh to blaze?

What if there was? What if there were no dragons then? What if we were children once and some small part of our lives stayed that way, summers of bright skies and flowers in the bush that held our hands? What if the days were clear and we could breathe in them? What if our homes were firm homes that didn't come crashing down when they were shouldered by a storm? What if we could walk all day in the streets and in the hills, never once looking over our shoulder or sniffing acrid notes in the air?

These days, we pat his orange feathers.

Always, he bites.

Surely You Can't Be Serious

Leslie Nielsen is stuck in traffic.

They're digging up the street, a garden bed of bitumen with white lines marking out unproductive rows. Constant ploughing, planting, cropping: he can't remember a time when the diggers weren't hammering their chins at the ground. He's been sitting there for years and the wheels have melted into the bitumen. The shoelaces of his car are tied to all the other cars, the traffic lights and buildings, and he feels like the whole city is just about ready to trip over and land in the river with the kind of splat you'd get if you swatted the moon from the sky.

A blackbird flies past with a wire in its beak. Leslie Nielsen's hair has gone brown and then white again. His suit has crumpled his skin. He wishes he could reach under the dash and pull out a siren, but this isn't a movie. Anyway – his siren would join the others screaming in the dust like a bunch of kids with grazed knees curled up and crying.

Leslie Nielsen groans, rubs his neck. He's forgotten where he is going, forgotten how to drive. Sometimes he thinks he'll forget his name. 'Leslie Nielsen,' he mutters to the rear-view mirror, frowning. There's a worker about twenty metres down the road wearing a hi-vis jacket and holding up a red sign, standing there like a dull sunset. It's a stop sign and Leslie Nielsen knows this because the roadworker never turns it around. He thinks for the hundredth time that he should get out of his car to see what the other side says, but that will be the moment the right lane opens and then bang, the streets will be locked up again forever.

He's going to be late, he supposes. Leslie Nielsen looks at the flowers on the passenger seat and hunts for a card. He's supposed to meeting someone. His wife? His mistress? He can't remember. Jerry Zucker? It has been too long. Years. When did he first get into the car?

Leslie Nielsen makes thinking kinds of faces. He's quite good at them; he checks the rear-view mirror. What about the one with the grimace?

There's a knock at his window and he jumps in surprise, whacking the mirror off kilter. Leslie Nielsen turns around, raises his eyebrows. A man is stepping back to the side of the road and holding out his thumb.

A hitchhiker? Leslie Nielsen's eyebrows form daisy chains with his hair. Can't the man see that he is stuck in traffic? Why wouldn't he just walk? Leslie Nielsen shrugs and points to the parade of spent cars. The hitchhiker looks pointedly at the empty seat with the flowers, then taps on the window again. He walks back to the edge of the street and sticks out his thumb.

Leslie Nielsen sighs.

Perhaps the footpaths are closed. The man could be killed by a grader or fall into a hole. He pushes open the door, adjusts the flowers, and the hitchhiker dives into the seat.

'Hi,' says the hitchhiker. He looks closer. 'Hey, aren't you Leslie Nielsen?'

Leslie Nielsen nods.

'Well, that's great! I always loved your films. I mean, I know they had their critics' – Leslie Nielsen frowns – 'but when Lucy died they just about kept me going.'

Leslie Nielsen smiles again.

As they sit there together, the man describes his favourite parts from each film. Not just the comedies – he loved *Forbidden Planet* and *The Poseidon Adventure*. Even *Tammy and The Bachelor*. Leslie Neilson doesn't remember that one but he grins wickedly and encourages the hitchhiker to go on. When did he last talk to another person? He'd honked – how many times he had honked – but talk? He's tempted to ease the car forward a centimetre or two, just for a treat. He's reserved a tiny gap between his car and the next for Christmas and Easter. He feels so cheered that he starts to think he might just about get wherever he's going.

But then he looks down at the flowers he moved to the dashboard.

One of them is missing. He checks again. Definitely only three. There had been four flowers. He would know; they'd been travelling with him for such a long time. He had named them after Beatles, had pitched them as seasons and cardinal directions. He'd dreamed up basketball sides where he played power forward and the flowers made up the numbers. He had liked the yellow rose for point guard. That's the one missing. He risks a sidelong glance at his companion.

The man is holding the yellow rose very carefully in his hands.

Leslie Nielsen frowns again. That's not right. You don't steal a man's flowers. But the hitchhiker is very engaging. He's talking about how much he and Lucy enjoyed *The Reluctant Astronaut*. Leslie Nielson hasn't thought of that film in years. He's taken back to the space program, the fire that killed the astronauts around the time it was released. He feels sad, and happy, and reflective. He drifts off, stares out the window at a digger that is emptying a hole and filling it back up again. He feels that he could just about make eye contact with the digger's operator, but he is distracted by a tiny movement to his right.

There are only two flowers on the windowsill. The man has taken the red tulip. That had been the small forward. You can't play basketball without a small forward. Leslie Nielsen isn't quite mad, and he isn't quite delighted. He doesn't know what to do. He could kick the man out for stealing his flowers, but what then? He'd be stuck in his car, all alone, till the end of time. Or he could wander down the path of old films he can barely remember until the hitchhiker takes all the flowers. But then the hitchhiker might get out of the car anyway, leaving him alone again; this time without flowers.

Leslie Nielsen grits his teeth. While he has been worrying and wondering, the man has taken the daffodil. It sits in a huddle with the rose and the tulip, bright and comfortable in their company.

They are careful in the man's hands and he is careful with them.

'Anyway,' the hitchhiker says, 'how about *Dayton's Devils?* I always thought you should be remembered for *Dayton's Devils.*'

Leslie Nielsen thinks so too, now the man has said it. To hell with the flowers. He doesn't need them. He's going nowhere. The flowers are useless. He should have torn them up and thrown them out the window years ago. He should have eaten them. Given them to the guy with the stop sign to hold up, just for something different. For a moment he thinks about getting out of the car for good, leaving it behind and walking back the way he came. Maybe everyone else has done that. Maybe this is why the man had been so insistent about riding with *him*. Maybe he's the last one left and the road is filled with the empty shells of cars. Could he even find his way home? Is it home he has been searching for? The man has taken the last flower now, a lily, and he doesn't care. He can't remember who the flowers are for.

Leslie Nielsen gives his companion an appraising look.

A thought sends his heart tumbling along like it is bouncing over speed bumps. He takes his foot off the clutch, eases back the handbrake, and caresses the accelerator with his big toe. The car moves forward just a fraction and the engine cheers.

The hitchhiker has all the flowers. But he has been talking about something else, and Leslie Nielsen feels like he should have been paying attention. His wife again, how much he misses her. The hitchhiker has tears in his eyes. He says that he wishes he could give her flowers like these. But the accident... anyway, he explains, that's why he has always been so thankful for the films. And the comedies! He hasn't even started on them. Watching *The Naked Gun,* he'd laughed for the first time in years, and he's grateful, hugely grateful, but – as he registers the change in angles and new perspectives – he explains that he has to get out.

'Wait!' says Leslie Nielsen, but the hitchhiker doesn't wait. He steps out of the car with the flowers and trudges over to something that

Leslie Nielsen has never seen before, a black pole with a red cross marked at the top. There is no rubble around it, just a tiny fist of grass. The hitchhiker gently places the flowers by the marker and walks on.

Leslie Nielsen looks through the blurred windscreen, tears in his eyes. All the roads are clear.

A Visitor's Guide to the Huts of Mount Wellington: 1913

Grass Tree Hut

Date Constructed: 1890
Constructed By: Arthur Wilson
Present Owner: Arthur Wilson
Size: 3 squares
Construction Materials: Hardwood, myrtle, convict brick
Site Location: 200 metres east, junction Sawmill Track and Dance's Track

Grass Tree Hut is the cleanest, most immaculate of huts. It was built by Arthur Wilson; his reputation suggests that while he always found a way to get his hands dirty, the hut provided a focus for his aspirations to homeliness. There is a neat, rectangular mat at the door, which we believe Wilson replaces every year to ensure that boot-brushed dust finds no means to stowaway.

We understand that initially, Wilson had expected hut etiquette to keep his table candle-wax free, that crumbs would be brushed carefully into hands and that coats would be left on the prominent hooks outside the door. ('Outside, in our rain weather? In all the forest *thisness?*' we wondered at the hut bylaw nailed politely to the boards outside the hut). In time, his high expectations proved beyond walkers' habits. He began to attach small signs to everything like a city council worried about litigation.

'Please leave coats outside.'

'Please leave your boots by the door.'

'Please use the cloths provided.'

There were dozens throughout the interior, and as with many ideologues, the laws began to seem more important to Wilson than the principles they were upholding. They had more than doubled since our last visit. It was disconcerting trying to find a place to sit down, as though by some unspoken infraction we were readying his pen to write another message of polite rebuke.

When we arrived, Arthur Wilson washed his hands and strode over to shake ours. His manner was hospitable, and despite our qualms we felt personally welcomed. 'Wonderful to see you again. I'm glad you were able to make it.' We didn't have to wait long before steaming mugs of tea were placed in the cool caves between our hands, tin cups that scalded and passed on their heat. Wilson told us about a famous visitor, a mountaineer well-known in Germany, and how the last *Guide* of 1904 had led to a profusion of such personages. He showed us the entries in his logbook.

'So,' he finally said, putting it to one side. 'It's been a long time. We're glad to see you back.' He was looking tired, bald with grey patches of hair above his ears, eyes narrowed by glasses. We craned our necks to look towards the roof. Grass Tree Hut, of course, is also known for its height. While it's not uncommon for Tasmanian huts to possess a small mezzanine gripping the wall, Grass Tree Hut is remarkable for its third story. We have no knowledge of the upper levels, as we have never been invited to climb them. Do the standards of tidiness persist, we wondered, or does leaf litter fall upwards, coating the third floor in handkerchiefs and dirty socks?

We imagine the crackling and screeching of possums alongside. We find the idea of sleeping among the brushing leaves attractive. We think about echoes, the sound of a boot thrown from the third floor.

'I tried to build a small mill,' Wilson explained, 'on the rivulet down the way. Never done it before, but I thought it would sustain the time. Not so different from carpentry. I always liked the thought of grinding wheat to flour. Well I was fool enough to use sandstone from the quarry. Not thinking clearly at all. My word, he said, 'that first batch was rough bread.'

We wished Arthur Wilson good morning. He nodded, and we brushed imaginary dust into our hands, straightening what we had crooked.

Forest Hut

Date Constructed: 1902
Constructed By: Samuel Cooper/David Stuart
Present Owner: David Stuart
Construction Materials: Hardwood, rock, convict brick
Site Location: 300 metres south of Octopus Tree

Forest Hut is the simplest of huts, reflecting many basic structures and ruins on higher plateaus, but surpassing them all for bare efficiency. It has no furniture that could be dragged out and auctioned, just a packed dirt floor, which may once have held flagstones squatting by the fire. A series of planks and stones are arranged as a shivering bed. 'There were bricks, but the chimney,' said David Stu, indicating the fire brewing in the corner, 'the chimney was never *found* enough and we had to keep finding it over and over again. Only the bricks helped us in the end.' Inside, the chimney is built of stones slotted together craftily. There are no bricks to be seen.

Outside, however, the chimney rises well beyond the hut's traditional structure and the bricks are to blame, grading upwards and outwards, ash leaking from the corners, a boxer's face smoking in the night. Any efforts that might have been made to renovate the insides have instead been pressed to service on the chimney. Forest Hut exemplifies two romantic notions reacting against each other: the sculpture growing in urban, rectangular angles; the branches and timber subsumed into nature.

We have always believed that David Stu had an eye to the future, a vision of hut fossils denuded of their rotten wood or burnt out by the fires. We felt that he had taken careful note of their remains, the towers rising from the plains, and wanted to ensure that his was a true Babylonian structure, a lasting image that would stand on its own foot. An exotic, Tasmanian *modernisme* twisting and clutching itself together, spread out and founded on a chimney.

At the sound of our hollow knock, David Stu raised the latch and shuddered the door open. He smiled sadly, as he always did, but boomed us into the hut with welcoming tones.

'Well, I didn't expect to be seeing you again. And another edition!' We sat on the ground; he settled the billy on the fire. 'As you can see, not a lot's changed. Bit more substance up top, I think we're slowly filling out where we need to be.' David Stu owned plenty of mugs, kept in a box with his tea, flour and other foundations under a rickety bed. Did he sleep on the bed? 'No,' he admitted. 'And I never have. Always in front of the fire.' So why did he keep it? 'You know I like things spare. Some say a hut without any furniture at all would be simpler. But is seven a simpler version of eight? Needs a bench or a bed in here so the hut can be what it is.'

David Stu is an absorbed man, and many find his ruminations difficult and off-putting. The delicate, finding luxuries absent, may be tempted to move on swiftly before they stain their locks and dresses. He has been this way as long as we have known him to dwell in Forest Hut. We don't pretend to understand the implications of his musings, but he is pleasant company. It didn't take long for the conversation to move on to birds and burrows. We enjoyed our tea and a biscuit or few, before travelling down the slope from his home of clarity.

Fern Retreat Hut

Date Constructed: 1890
Constructed By: Alan Duffield
Present Owner: Alan Bally
Construction Materials: Hardwood, sheoak, blackwood, myrtle, Huon pine, fossilised wood

Fern Retreat Hut was first titled Fern Hut by its creator Alan Duffield, but his successor, his cousin Alan (species Bally), enabled its true nature to unfold by adding the word 'retreat'. The name that greets rare visitors does not commemorate any defensive or rear-guard manoeuvre (the hut has courageously seen many storms evaporate against its walls), but its hiddenness. Fern Retreat Hut seems to tuck itself into a thicket of fronds, and it is the most difficult of huts to find.

There is the problem of the route. Some say the track begins thirty-eight guideposts from the first turn, others forty-seven. Either can take you into the vicinity. Equally, either path can direct you into circular wanderings and pademelon feet. Fern Retreat Hut is never announced by its roof, the manner by which many of the more brazen cabins call attention to themselves. The phenomenon of stumbling on shelters is well known; they are nowhere, they are ten minutes, half an hour away, then suddenly the painting is on the wall and there are promises of warmth and rest. If anything, Fern Retreat Hut is only noticed after stumbling upon it, after you are already inside and Bally is pouring you tea. When did you knock? A tree has slid aside. A cave has been unlocked behind camouflaging branches.

Fern Retreat Hut is also the only hut we know of that is made entirely of wood: walls, joinery and fireplace. Heating is said to have been left off the original design, but bowing to winter necessity, it was later constructed entirely from lengths of fossilised timber, ancient gums mined and stacked in hardwood silence.

This is not fanatical. There are tin mugs, stainless steel knives and the flesh of Bally's hands reaching out to grip our own, welcoming us inside and seeing us seated.

'Found the place then,' he said and grinned. 'Take you long?' We admitted that even with prior visits and scrawled maps, our hasty confidence had been betrayed by the stubbornness of the hut's position. Bally loved his forest wood, but he loved the retreat more, and this is what he wanted to hear. We were glad that it was able to be true.

Given the hour, Bally was kind enough to offer us fresh damper and we eagerly joined him, doughing up sticks and fishing against the fire. The smell freshened the hut, bathing it in a new warmth, and the quiet owner opened up.

'Regulations, there are no regulations, even the mapping people don't want to poke their noses in here. Arbitrary, I think, what they square. Never seen them myself.' We suggested that even with a map, people would find it difficult to reach the hut. He nodded: 'Always thought so myself. Everyone knows roughly where it is. You get the odd expeditioner, one who needs to plant a flag and they're welcome, but it doesn't mean they'll find the place next time. Like you.' We wondered about a rumour that he somehow moves Fern Retreat Hut every couple of years. 'Not true. Any other place would be easier to find than the bottom of this well. Duffield had it right. Enough about me, anyway. How are your daughters coming along?' The damper was ready, the smell thickened the air and blended with the sawdust sticking to our faces. There was jam, blackberry, and we presented a little cheese for the feast. New minds and muscles possessed us. 'Do you like the smell?' Bally asked, breathing in forcefully.

Stepping out from the door, we managed to resist the urge to turn around and peer into the bush, to search for the hut we had just left.

Falls Hut

Date Constructed: 1897
Constructed By: Magda Slein
Present Owner: Magda Slein

Falls Hut is beautiful, or at least is found to be beautiful where it is found. It stands in a noisy glade, between two sets of falls that merge into one rivulet below the hut before splitting in a gully downstream, as though the hut was magnetised for water.

There are no bridges across the streams. You have to jump, rock-hop or get your ankles wet, and there is a near constant mist condensing from the force of water falling. It is perhaps the daily moisture in this damp site that has darkened and warped Falls Hut in small ways, plucking nails, bending boards and making it appear older than it is. This wrangling has encouraged leaks in the roof that are managed with strategic tarps and flies.

Surprisingly, this was all foreseen by the builder of Falls Hut, Magda Slein, who in contrast to the brick epitaph envisaged by David Stu, decided to accept a certain level of destruction in order to avoid a more complete one. She allied her dwelling with the element of water in a continuous defence against the omnivorous fires that strike these hills every time the summer wind turns north-west. In this location, bounded and soaked by fluid, a cup cradled in the clay soil, Magda hoped to be shielded from a catastrophic blaze churning up the gums.

You might imagine a certain discomfort — mouldering clothes, wrinkled pasty skin and a leech for every limb – but in reality, if you swim through the site, you'll find that thanks to its generous host, Falls Hut is the most hospitable of huts. Draped in waterproof fabrics inside and out, it evokes images of an oriental boudoir, and the fire takes care to blast all moisture from the rugs that coat the floor. Think not of dark, damp carpets and their smell, but of straw, dry cotton, and the best wool scratching and teasing your feet. All moisture is blasted to the other side of each plank, which may explain its particular grotesqueries. The hut is two-faced, wet and dry according to where you stand.

Magda was delightfully open and grey, huddling us in with warmth and fresh afternoon scones. There are few scones as delicious as Magda's, steaming like the tea, filling us after the longer journey from our last port of call. 'My loves,' she said. 'So lovely and so sad. Come and sit a while.' Had things changed here? 'Not at all,' she replied. 'Though I wonder at times if the planks are twisting so much the whole place will turn inside out. As if the outside wants a turn against the fire. But no, it's still the same. Look,' she showed us to the logbook. 'Here's your last visit, so nice to see all of you then.'

We were getting tired, and perhaps a little sloppy, but Magda had always been gracious and forgiving. A long day. We were grateful for every drop of tannin staining our drinks.

Clematis Hut

Date Constructed: 1890s
Present Owner: Sarah de Winter

Clematis Hut is renowned as a place of transience. Nobody is known to have ever stayed the night. It's provenance is unknown; it may have been constructed thousands of years ago for all the record shows, but this does not account for its lack of visitors. Yes, it is awkward, well out of the way of most walkers on the other side of the mountain in a wide patch of scree; partly scree itself, with rolled stone walls and darkness. But Clematis Hut is no day shelter, no square with a table, hosting picnics when rain governs proceedings. There is no sign prescribing a diurnal function, no fines or bylaws. There is even a wide, sunken bench that has too much girth to be purely for seating.

It is a bed, but a bed never slept in. The logbook records only day visitors, and few enough of them. Perhaps people choose not to leave a written record, as though fearing they are writing on stone.

We have never met Sarah de Winter, despite our best efforts, and we are not confident that she is a regular visitor to her own hut. We have been known to wonder if she is some kind of historical accident, a name inscribed in a book found in a musty attic.

We did not linger in Clematis Hut. While the sun hadn't set, we were aware of the mountain's shade.

Cave Hut

Present Owner: Phil Walker

Cave Hut is the smallest of huts, but it is no coffin resting on a hillside. Cave Hut is built beside a small cliff face, though 'cliff' is actually too high a word, as the rock extends just an arms-length beyond the hut, for which it provides a southern wall. There is just enough room for two benches, one above the other, and a recessed fireplace that glows quietly in the corner.

Cave Hut wasn't built with visitors in mind. It's a fishing bolt-hole, a resting place for those driving highland stock, an emergency shelter for those who ski or walk for recreation. A thumb pressed into the side of the forest, cosy and quiet enough to pour the rain and wind from your back. And, though small and slightly awkward, Cave Hut has the reputation of being the quietest, most restful of huts. There's no room for great gatherings around a wide-boarded table, no roasts circling on a spit. Just the outside, a small clearing with chainsawed logs arranged as stools, or in bad weather, the bunks to lie against and sleep.

Necessity obliges all visits to be relatively brief; it's only a close friend who stays the night as an invited guest. All the restless aspire to an invitation, those who know Phil Walker and like him, or hope that they would like him, and he's selective about who he chooses for the privilege.

'Love to offer you the night,' he said. 'Getting on, too. Place would probably do you good.' We assured him we had other plans. We were sitting on the stumps outside, watching the night creep across the sky. 'You eaten?' he asked. The fire was burning in a pile of stones. He asked if we were well, if we were all okay.

Phil Walker is not a big man, but he likes to sit outside and enjoys keeping to himself. We commented on how late it was getting and how, despite his protests, it was probably time to leave him to the evening.

Fernlea Hut

Fernlea Hut belongs to no one, but tonight it belongs to us. We are staying the night, through all the mash of sound and light in the bush. The rules are written in simple code at the back of this logbook, in pictures and cuneiform script. No one knows we are here, we have told no one and we will discuss this fact. We will discuss the rules and we will honour them. We will pull up the ladder that leads to the base of this hut and we will mount a guard to watch for any eavesdroppers.

We are allowed to light two candles.

Two candles are lit.

Fernlea Hut was never built, it was only ever being built, and now and then we will add a branch or frond like a walker throwing rocks to a cairn. It is high, high on the _____ Ridge, along _____ Track below the mountain. There are branches across the track junction, enough to seem part of the bush edging. There is an old well along the track that could be a hole, and a few flattened areas that may once have held huts in their palms. We do not know what happened to them. There is no corrugated iron as in other ruins, no flattened metal that shows where an old hut was squashed below great feet.

There is a set of gloves waiting on a rock near the small rivulet.

Tonight we are together. It is colder than we anticipated. We shift closer to the two candles. Blankets are firm around our shoulders and we reach for the chocolates that we have brought. There is treasure to be found in Fernlea Hut tonight.

Be My Dora

Here we are, dropped by a filthy blue minibus in the middle of a flat wasteland with sick looking shrubs, and we have to cross the river. There's nowhere to sleep; this is the side that floods. The river floods every time the rain squabbles with the hills and all the spill runs away crying.

Twelve boats wait like apostles berthed in the silt, and all of them are named *Dora*. 'Pete,' says Griselda, gripping my arm. 'Dora is *everywhere*.'

It's true. My mother, my sister and three ex-girlfriends. If there is a Dora in the world I'm connected to them somehow. Griselda is frowning at the boats as though they have splits in their hulls that will drink us down to the bottom of the river; as though they will forget the wind and follow serious currents into rapids, waterfalls and widening seas. The letters are painted in a rough black script on the sterns; also on the angles of the bows. Griselda wrinkles her nose and looks up and down the river for a bridge. She checks her phone.

'I think I'll build a boat,' she says.

'The workshops are on the other side of the river,' I offer.

'I reckon it would be easy.' Griselda picks up a piece of cardboard that is covered with pictures of bananas and a black stain that may once have been a banana; the cardboard is a little muddy and torn. She gives it a little shake and some of the dirt falls off.

She brightens.

One of the boatmen coughs and wanders a little closer. 'Excuse me,' he says. 'Do you need a ride across the river? It's a good boat. Hell cheap.'

'No thank you,' says my girlfriend.

'Griselda...' I start.

'We're fine,' she says, cutting me off. 'Hey look, why is your boat called *Dora*?'

The boatman seems puzzled.

'If it was your mother's name, I get it. But so many mothers named Dora?'

I should explain that this is nothing like the Griselda I love. The Griselda who came knocking at my door in the tumbling rain to explain I had left the headlights on in my car, who wouldn't give up even though I had a Pejačević symphony amplified so courageously, until finally I heard the plaintive, persistent knocking and opened the front door to see her saturated. 'Lights,' she gasped, 'car.' I asked her in and offered her a cup of tea. She thought for a moment. 'I'm your neighbour,' she replied, as though it were a word of caution or warning, that I had better not do anything stupid or presume on her person, because I should know that her house next door would be listening with its chimneys pricked up, ready to smash open its door and leap upon me like a German Shepherd if anything was to threaten its beloved mistress – and because after all, we were neighbours – and so she sat down in front of the bar heater that was smelling of burning dust and I brought her a cup of warm milk sweetened with leatherwood honey, and she told me she had been visiting her little brother and was getting worried, because his eyes seemed frosted to the screen all day, and we talked for a few hours as the battery in my car went completely and utterly dead.

'Miss,' says the boatman sadly, as a trickle of wind blows the dust up against our legs. 'Dora' is our word for 'boat'. This is why you see all of my friends with the same name. It is impossible to cross the river without a dora.'

Griselda throws down the cardboard and sits on a rock.

I don't know what to do.

The Doras had never bothered her till we started travelling. 'It's not even my middle name,' she had complained in an old Jewish cemetery in Sofia. Later, I caught her eyeing my body for tattoos, burrowed under my arms or hidden between my toes. But if she found the guilty letters, what then?

I have never stumbled over her name. She has always been Griselda, even late at night and early in the morning.

But over the last week we have stopped talking, buried in our books and our phones like trains in tunnels; rocks and mountains blocking the space between us. Every morning I have been expecting to wake up in our hostel and find her bed filled with a dreadlocked Swede fiddling with his phone and smelling of the previous month. This was my last hope; a golden resort beside a soothing river with honey in the air and cocktails in the trees. We would dance at midnight in a rug of the moon's soft light; we would hold hands at a table and keep holding them.

But all of that is a river away, and now the boatman has returned to his fellows. They are smoking and stare past us. The evening is making for twilight and each glowing cigarette is a tiny sunset over the water. It is not beautiful. It is getting cold and heavy rain is forecast.

I sit down beside Griselda. There is only one rock, so I hunch on the ground as the chill reaches into my back. Griselda says something quietly and I don't catch it. The sound of the river is gritty, as though it is flowing with lead. There is a new power in it, a strength and determination that paddles up from the banks and hisses in our ears.

'What?' I ask. 'What was that?'

'Do you want me to change my name?' she repeats in a low, flat voice.

'Of course not,' I reply, reaching my arm around her body, trying to draw her close; but this would pull her off the rock so her body tenses up and I leave it as a loose, unsettling hug.

One by one the boatmen disappear across the river, until the one who spoke to us is left. He looks up at the clouds that are clustering around the hills like sheep; throws a spent cigarette into the river. 'Listen,' he calls over to us. 'I'm Sammy. I have a son, two daughters, about your age. Bit younger. Anyway, don't worry about the money.

I've got to get home with this weather. Looks bad. I'll take you over for nothing. Hop in.'

The clouds are dark and it is not just the evening coming on. There is a misting in the air which isn't quite resolving into droplets.

'Griselda,' I say.

'I'm staying,' she says.

'It's going to rain,' I say. 'It's pretty much raining now.'

'I don't mind the rain,' she replies. 'Let it bloody rain.'

For a moment it seems the boatman wants to gather us in his arms; as though he is remembering his children when they were younger and played too close to the river; then he looks as if he wants grab at our bodies and drag us to his boat, scolding us all the way. But he remembers who he is, who we are, and turns his face to one side in a kind of shrug. Body follows chin like ship to a rudder, and he pads back down to the mounting waves, heaves the boat on to the water, splashes in and rows with strong, even strokes.

As he blurs into the mist, the rain starts to thump down properly and I begin to feel frightened. Frightened of the word 'flood'; the images of dark water and homes, of whole towns submerged, of desperate people waving from rusting roofs. I want to hurry as far from the river as I can, leap across the plains like an antelope; but Griselda is here and she is still and certain. My hair wets into strands and then my jacket darkens. My skin feels pale and she is still sitting there on that red rock as though she is part of the foreshore. 'You know,' she finally says, as we gaze across the river at the resort's flashy glow barely picking its way through the heavy curtains of cloud, 'you've left the lights on again.'

The river begins to rise, quicker than we could have imagined. It spills out across the floodplain and runs over small obstacles; sniffs at our shoes and then leaps across our ankles; there is sudden mud below our feet and the water bites at our legs as it climbs towards our knees, cold claws pressing into our skin as it tries to drag us out. We let go of our bags and watch as they spin into the current – and at what point, I wonder, did this hug of comfort blend into such clinging?

I don't want to laugh as the water lifts us up and tickles at our bodies and I don't want to cry as the river begins to pull us downstream.

I want to be strong and reliable and always floating.

Griselda's voice is in my ear.

'Pete,' she whispers. 'Be my *dora*. Be my boat.'

What Fear Was

where no farmers had ploughed the trees or settled seeds to graze the soil, where the folded arms of scrub bar gullies, where the wide buttongrass plains swelter under peaks of old quartz, there, a boy with his hands and a girl with her feet went out to learn what fear was; their coats on and off, steady offerings calming the drizzle, the evening tiring out and resting as they waded the cool creek, ducked below mosquitoes and planted their tent, pouring torches over the fuel stove that sat bubbling water into dusty grub, the climb, said the girl with her feet, I can't see it being much of a problem, and the boy with his hands nodded, no way, and the dry lightning sounded in the air as the clouds found few tears; just as we dangle our eyes across the drying grass, useless golden grass, the parched tomatoes and papery corn, this is not the colour of our island but the westerlies have drummed the moisture out, our hollow backyard rivulet with its ferns fading ill and the evergreens flushing autumn, the shells of marsupials chewing edgy stones and the water tank fasting through another hot day when we take to the blank, startled beaches, the salt water infested with bodies, while others hurtle for the high country, the argument of mountains that the boy with his hands and the girl with her feet stared down an hour's trudge away through the dense heat wallowing in the plains, sweat washing through their shirts and their hair and sunscreen stinging their eyes, step-step buried in the grasping mud, packs pressing thumbs through their shoulders, punching in their tailbones, drink, they said, have a drink, fine, they said, no worries, as they climbed through the roots of the moraine, resting under hung rocks with moist soaks thirsting green, look, the red christmas bells flowering, look, the view across pedder to an orphaned peak, look, as they struggled over the ridge's relief, as they threw their loads against the grass and floated, look, look, smoke. A great pillar of smoke in the south-west. And so the boy with his hands on his hips and the girl with her feet shrivelled inside her boots, who went out to learn what fear was, fumbled their eyes on distant coals, the wind flying the ash flag well to the south, should be okay, the girl said, better up here than down in the valley, it's a long way off, but as they stretched out to the lake their eyes remained skinned on the sky's stain; and we with our minutes swum in the river's sharp water are jogging to the car, towels askew and surrounded by news, we are driving home staring at the eucalypts piled up the hill, the radio hearkening for reports and warnings, maps expanding online, the phone alert and ready, there is smoke pouring over the back of the mountain and we focus on the same, same bulletins, our stations at the window, white air, grey skin, the haze that hovered around the cygnus cirque as the boy with his hands and the girl with her feet inched through the jagged teeth snapping at the sky, posed on the rims edging the world, low lakes nesting under pale rocks, and on the drop to a shallow tarn they met a wombat scuttling uphill, where you going? the wombat asked, and the boy with his hands explained about their full traverse, heading out then? he asked, and the wombat blurred her ears back and yeah, no views here, it's rubbish, should be right to head on, keep plenty worried water for tomorrow, and they strode forwards, finding and losing the vista in steep gullies and the slow spreading smoke, until two wallabies hurtled past them, pulled up and turned, munching by the everlasting daisies and the spread of alpine richeas, what do you reckon, they asked, anything to worry about? and the girl with her feet, staring and admiring their elongated paws, said, we don't know what fear is, just keep going I reckon, us too said the roos, we're heading all the way to feder, five days we hope, we'll be right, hope we'll be alright, as we stew and swot the scrawled notes tacked to the kitchen's wooden wall, computers first and then the chooks, and if we have time heap the paintings and the books and the clothes in the back of the car and streak for the road down to town, though if the road is sliced take off to the south, and if we see it growing on the hilly ridge just jump for the car and go, go, so many dry and windy days, we remember when the trees were gentle, holding hands and idling, where have they gone, where has it got to now wondered the boy and the girl on a bright bride of a morning that was quickly turning bleary as they stamped the slow leg, fishing packs up cliffs with the rope biting their bruised fingers, creeping through burrows in the roofs of caves, the smoke was to the north and to the south as the white flecks of ash rained silently in the loitering breeze, closer, the beast was closer and they were locked on the range, closer, should they flow back to the chill lake or drop and rush for the dam, should they keep along the route to the high moor, does it burn, they wondered, can it get a clean grip on the alpine turf, and they listened to the rattling of helicopters, echoes slapping off the cliffs, the smell of soot in their clothing, keep climbing and if there's danger then surely, surely they'll be gathered in arms and carried up from red clutches over the olive map, fine, we'll be fine, we hope in our cabin on the outskirts of town as the repeated roar of choppers crackles the evening, our thoughts filled with bursting valleys and flat yards, scorched fences, faces under jetties and rust in the leaves and the air as it leaps through the canopy and rips homes to pieces, darkness painted on the land, and lying in tentative sheets, rhythm shuddering the night air, we are worried, we are fearful, we are scared

Here Are the Holes in My Eyes

1.

Nobody can explain the leaks. They are springing from every runnel in the corrugated iron roof and dribbling through the ceiling. All the cupboards are empty. Every bowl, pot and spoon has been strategically arranged around Miles' house.

The hallway, the bedrooms and the living room.

The office and the kitchen.

The bathroom and laundry have been left to fend for themselves. Miles has run out of crockery and he's not going to cater for the cousins of cousins just to keep all those drips off the floor for an extra couple of hours.

2.

Miles has been on the roof and he was careful. He stepped on the bolts or the screws; whatever you call those metal fingers that grip the failing steel. He was wary around the edges. He has heard that ninety-eight percent of the men of his age who turn up to emergency departments have fallen off their roofs. He wonders if his home has turned sieve just to lure him up, if it will buck and shake, push him over the edge.

Miles doesn't find any obvious gashes in the metal. There is plenty of silicone bandaging up the gaps where bolts, screws or nails have penetrated its skin. Miles places a patch of gaffer tape over every one of them, just to be sure. The tape is black, firm, and confident. It makes claims.

But the roof continues to leak.

3.

The house has been soaked for nearly three weeks. The leaks started on a clear day in the new year while Miles was trying to get the exact wording right on a letter to his father. He was straining, his forehead was lined and sweat blanketed his body. As he crossed out words and then wrote them again, the paper was beginning to resemble the cut-out of an ant farm; so many black scribbles in the sand. He leaned back, rubbed his neck, and a single drop of water fell.

Miles was aware of it obliquely, as though its trail through the air ran just near the corner of his eye, even though it was falling directly before him. As he focused properly, it seemed to hang there, reflecting the beige walls, the couch, his mug of cooling coffee and his face – for a brief instant his face – and then it splattered and sank into the page he was working on. And then another fell, and another, and then a stream of water blurred the paper and the ink. He scrunched up the ruined letter and threw it towards the bin; adjusted his mug below the leak, shifted his position, found another sheet of paper and tried to begin again.

4.

There had been a long weekend. Miles and his brothers had taken a long-planned summer trip to the government huts in the mountains. They'd wanted to get out together, take a day walk to one of the peaks and see what guidance the views had to offer. His youngest brother, Sam, had wanted to find the Erratics, two large, square boulders sitting in the middle of a valley as if they had wandered in, found a place to lounge and then made themselves comfortable with a camp fire burning between them; the boulders leaning over, cooking up wallabies and warming themselves in the heat. In the evening the brothers had hoped to sit by their own flames, work their way through a few bottles of red, wrap a couple of beefy spuds in foil and blacken them in the coals.

But it had rained all through the weekend, a heavy grey rain from the south-west that drummed its dull fingers on the roof and darkened the floor. The three brothers had circled the small lake and gotten totally soaked, and that was about enough walking; instead, they bound themselves to the hut as the heater chain-smoked through the timber and they stewed and worried and drained the grog. On the Saturday night, when Miles volunteered to make a trip down the gravel road to the pub to resupply, they all decided to come; the prospect of a counter meal in the warm light too tempting. And so they hurried from their lonely hut to the car and its lights had pressed down the gravel road.

The brothers sat around the brown formica table in the pub, feeling they had somehow betrayed their trip and its purpose; albeit feeling content with fresh beers and porterhouse steaks. It had been the smart, ruthless course of action. As their plates and glasses emptied the brothers looked to each other – Miles to Sam, and Sam to the middle brother, Tony.

'Well,' said Miles, 'what do you think we should do about him?'

When he got home on the Monday evening to clear weather, Miles sat down at his table. When the first drips began to fall against the letter he was writing, he wondered if he had managed to stain the house with his damp weekend, as though the rain had snuck in together with his boots, his pack and his coat; as though it was seeking a certain justice or retribution for their lack of courage, their abdication of duty.

Their hut had been a post, and they had abandoned it without even thinking.

They had been heartless.

5.

The early leaks migrated swiftly. First one drip, and then two, and then a dozen, and then the whole living room was a mess of drizzle trickling into every crevice, saturating the carpet and the cushions. The rooms of the house fell one by one, despite Miles' best efforts to line the ceiling with tarpaulins and tent flies; to identify and capture every new puncture with a bucket and a squirt of sealant. The pots were constantly spilling over. It was a juggling act to keep track of them all, and Miles had to go to work. He had to collapse into his damp bed. As time passed he found that he stopped caring; just let the frying pans and speckled mugs brim and then splutter all over the carpet.

A dam was cracking, failing; it was bursting, and Miles had only so many fingers to poke into the crumbling wall.

6.

Miles has had all the experts around to the place that he can think of. A plumber, a builder, an expert meteorologist. They all just shake their heads. The builder tries to make light of Miles' situation. 'Did you read the contract properly? Are you sure you bought a house, you know, and not a fountain?' The builder grins as he waits for Miles to reply. 'A *fountain*,' he repeats.

Miles gives up on consulting experts. He finally rings his brother Tony, the most practical man he knows. When they were younger, Tony was putting together working engines out of scraps of rusty metal and fixing the wings of broken blackbirds. But when he answers the phone, Tony sighs and says that of course, he would come and have a look in normal circumstances, but he's having trouble with his daughter at the moment – yes, more trouble, the same thing, the food thing – and you know, he's had the odd leak around his own place that he hasn't been totally sure about.

'Do you think you maybe just move out for a while, mate?' he asks. 'Actually, you might kill two birds there, you know what I mean. Have you gotten around to having a word to him yet?' And Miles says that he hasn't, that he was planning to get a chance after they'd gone away to the mountains, but then all this trouble had started with the house and the leaks, and so he had put it on the back-burner for a while till that got sorted.

Was there absolutely no way that Tony was able to come over, talk things through, think about how best to deal with the situation?

'Sorry mate,' says Tony, 'I'm really snowed at the moment, but look, if it's still pouring down next week give us another call and we'll see what we can do.'

7.

Miles likes the idea of making the best of a bad situation, so he scatters seeds around the house and opens the curtains and the windows wide to let the sun breathe into the new growth. He has assigned the living room to flowers, to poppies, marigolds and pansies; in the kitchen, he has thrown packets of rocket and radish seeds, kale and mizuna. He has never been a successful gardener, but he feels that the conditions in his house are finally on his side.

Miles waits anxiously, wishing that something, somewhere, will grow up green and hopeful, but he can only watch as the seeds squat in the pools of water while white and black moulds spread across the shades of carpet, smothering and overcoming the early shoots like a bushfire raging across trembling fields.

8.

Eventually Miles takes Tony's advice. He sets up a tent inside the house, but after one wet night he realises it is simpler to put it on the patch of lawn out the back and make sure all the essentials that haven't already been ruined are stored comfortably in the shed. A lot of the electrical stuff is a write-off and the couches have had it, but he had shifted out some basics early on and double-bagged most of the important things. He likes to sit there in the dry tent with the photo album.

During the night, as he turns on aching hips and wakes for the eighth time, and as he listens to the possums squabble in the yard, he thinks about checking in to a hotel and living in dry comfort for a week; imagines his pale, wrinkled skin ironing out, the lightness of his clothes. But when morning dawns the thought has evaporated. The expense is one thing, and he quite enjoys the morning light looming through the fabric of the tent, but more than that, he worries that if he moves to another building with pretensions to stability and sturdiness, the leaks will simply follow him, folded in the pockets of his overnight bag, ready to burst out and storm down as soon as he pops it on the fresh, crisp seats.

9.

One morning Miles is woken by a series of creaks, and when they blend with his dreams he believes that they are the sound of his body struggling to hold itself together. As they persist, he catches hold of wakefulness and realises that they are coming from his house, as though it is groaning or weeping at its burden of water, as though the house has been filled entirely and is about to burst in an explosion of moisture, or lift off its foundations and float away on the surge of a river of its own making.

He unzips the tent and pokes his head outside into the early light. There is a breeze blowing from the direction of the house and he can smell the rot that is overtaking it, as though he is standing at the shore and there are piles of seaweed decomposing before him. The house moans again and he can sense the way its bones are cracking and pulling apart, and he feels a horrible sense of pity, of utter, powerless pity, and he realises that he is crying, that tears are rushing down his face, tears that cannot be stopped, tears that pulse and ripple across his cheeks and stain his shirt and his sleeping bag, that pool on the tent floor and dribble out on to the lawn, and no matter how much he tries to drag them back in there is nothing, absolutely nothing he can do to plug them up.

The Day the Music Died

We have to catch a plane but all morning we have been battling flies. Flies that gravel up our windows and fly when we want them to crawl, cry when we want them to die. We slap their leering faces and they sprawl on the carpet like twists of dark wool.

Reinforcements sneak in through gaps in the screen doors.

'Josh,' says Laura. 'What have you done?'

We grapple with them all morning. One dives into Laura's coffee; another sips at her poached egg. We sweep the bodies of dead flies into piles on the linoleum and set fire to them. Still they come, crashing and bouncing off the windows; the house filling up with black foam.

'Leave them,' says Laura. 'We're going to be late.' We heave our bags into the car. Park at the airport, check our luggage, print our passes, hunt down the gate. The televisions are on: disasters. A flood in Mexico and a building on fire, also in Mexico.

'There's time for a coffee,' says Laura. She strides over to the counter and I stare at the queue forming as the flight staff pick up microphones and put them down again.

~

We are going away, travelling overseas for the first time in years. Once, we chased nations for nine months, bellowing with bulls in the streets of Spain, squaring our eyes in countless galleries and flushing our minds in India. We returned, settled down, bought a house.

Now we are travelling to Fiji. Beaches that will smile, glowing water that will let us paddle without protest; water that won't even splash. It will be wonderful. We will be happy. The queue begins to lengthen and it's then I see the musicians. They're tucked in a corner of the lounge in old-fashioned suits. One young man with ruffles of curls and thick dark glasses. Another with a rugby build and a fifties crew-cut balanced on his head. The third, also stocky, living on the edge of his teens. They carry their guitars and I wonder why they haven't been checked. Their guitars won't fit in the overhead compartment. They won't fit under the seat in front.

Is this the inflight entertainment? Did I pay extra for this?

Laura rejoins the queue with her takeaway coffee. It is so big that I wonder if it is a milkshake and then I see how tired she is looking.

'We're on our way,' I try to grin, and reach for her arm.

She sways away, takes a huge slurp from her coffee. 'Somehow,' she says, and fiddles in her pocket for the boarding pass.

The flight staff are friendly; they have just come from Fiji. We find our seats and fuss around, making sure we have everything we need. We place our magazines and books in the pockets like survival rations and study the movie guide.

'We could watch something together,' I suggest. Laura frowns and reaches for a magazine.

When the musicians get on the plane there is a gentle murmur through the crowd. There is no first-class section, but they sit at the front of the plane as though separated by a thin pane of glass. Laura looks up. The guitars stick up above the seats, curious giraffes. The musicians cradle them like babies.

'Who's that?' she asks. There is a sudden tremor in her voice, like the wind is already whistling.

'Dunno,' I say. 'Maybe they got a special deal, couldn't check their kit cause it'd get trashed down below. Twang! Imagine that.'

Like a posing rock band smashing its guitars.

'We're going to crash,' says Laura.

A small flurry of snow trickles down my spine and flutters out into the plane.

'What do you mean?' I feel myself blinking quickly.

'They're back.' says Laura.

'Who's back?' I ask. 'What are you talking about?'

'They're going to try again.' She hums the opening chords of a song I barely recognise. 'Peggy Sue'? Somehow it morphs into 'La Bamba'.

'No way,' I say. 'We'll be fine. This is Qantas.'

'Maybe they've been given another chance,' says Laura.

The snow is still chilling my back. 'Fiji,' I remind her.

'Yes,' she says, calming a little. 'Fiji.'

'Flies,' I say.

'No,' she says. 'Yes, flies. Okay, look, just leave it then.'

Laura turns the pages of her magazine quickly, works through it again from the beginning. I'm worried too. But it is probably not those musicians and we are in our seats and the plane is beginning to taxi.

Soon we are in the air and we are whispering together.

'Do you remember,' I say, 'that time at uni when there was a dead dog lying in the gutter outside our house, and it was almost impossible to see the dog, because it was covered with flies?'

'I wanted to look closer,' says Laura.

'You wanted to look closer.' We were both squeamish about those things, but the flies had covered the dead body with a kind of modesty.

'Well, what about it?' asks Laura.

'Well, I don't know if I want to look any closer,' I say. 'Let's just get to this island.'

'We might still crash,' says Laura.

'We might crash,' I acknowledge. 'We probably will crash with those musicians on the plane, but let's cross that bridge when we come to it.'

The first round of service comes through. This time we both order coffee even though Laura hasn't finished hers. 'It's a long flight,' she says. 'Don't hassle me.' One or two people have gone to sleep and some are plugged into their films, but we are getting the sense that others are noticing the musicians. The weather outside is minus fifty degrees centigrade and we are travelling at nine hundred kilometres per hour. The musicians don't move from their seats. They don't ask for anything to eat or drink. Their entertainment screens are blank. We are ninety minutes into our flight; a line curves against the map. The musicians don't reach into their baggage for the mints they have forgotten. They don't stretch. We have travelled eleven hundred kilometres since leaving the airport. Someone goes up for an autograph, hesitates, pushes out a pen. They are gently rebuffed. There are two thousand eight hundred kilometres to go.

Rumours are whirring up and down the aisle. We don't listen to them.

'The thing that I would like,' says Laura suddenly. 'Is if you could smuggle an ice-cream container of sand from one of the beaches back in your luggage, and then if we could just sprinkle it all over the house, so that we barely notice it.'

'Okay,' I say. 'We can try that. I reckon they have heaps of ice-cream in Fiji. But sand is pretty heavy. It will have to be dry sand.'

'Dry sand is fine,' she says.

'Do you think you'll feel like going back to work?' I ask.

Laura looks intently at her magazine.

'Let's just start with the sand,' she says.

'I don't want to argue,' I say. 'It would be stupid to argue if the plane is going to crash.'

'It's not the time,' she says. 'You've never been good with the time. Focus on the sand.'

～

The rumours are getting a little louder and they are beginning to drown out the engine noise. There are last phone calls to loved ones and solicitors. People are making up, making love in their seats. But there's also a certain underdog confidence that is willing the musicians to make it this time. At some point the captain makes an announcement about the weather in Suva, the safe prevailing winds and their safe airline's famous safety record and their expert crew trained in safety and of course the safe complimentary beverages they are beginning to distribute. And then he cosies up to the musicians as though they are moody gods – 'I love that early rock and roll, Dad used to play it when we were kids' – as if they are in some way responsible for whatever course events will take. The musicians do not seem to react in any way. Their guitars remain still, periscoped above their seats.

Everyone is beginning to get a little drunk on the best booze the airline can offer. A light festival atmosphere flicks back the fear.

'I just think,' I begin, knowing I should be letting the sand trickle. 'I mean, I just want to say that I think we made the right decision.'

Laura looks up from her seat and begins to reply, but her voice drops away as the first engine fails.

The plane lurches.

'Well,' she says. 'So much for Fiji.'

The second engine fails and the plane begins a steepening dive. We cling to each other, restricted by our belts. The seatbelt indicator is on and perhaps if we had the strength to disobey and leap into each other's arms it would say something about our relationship. As it is, we twist and hold each other as the belts snarl at our waists. Around us there is a frenzy of terror or celebration. We are going to crash into the ocean and the water will leap and then it will settle down, and we will all be very still.

But the musicians rise from their seats.

They are so young.

They walk across to the cockpit, open the door, and begin to play their guitars.

There are no familiar rhythms or beats, just a long drone, a roar of primal vowel that monotones down the aisle like the engine of a plane; or perhaps a mass of flies hurling themselves about a room. And incredibly, the plane begins to stabilise. There is a new pressure in our backs, a reassuring pressure that settles our screams and pushes out our panic.

Laura lets go of my hand.

The musicians keep playing and we level out and start to rise. As the plane closes in on safety, the party swells, our fellow passengers cheering like they are at a concert; they are dancing in the aisles, twirling each other about, and they seem so delighted and relieved, as though a war has ended and they have run out into the streets. But as I rise and start to pull Laura from her seat to join the celebrations, she leans back against my grip and remains where she is.

'It's not that I'm ungrateful,' she says. 'But you know, Josh, it's not music they're playing.'

An Anti-Glacier Book

'You know what I say to people when I hear they're writing anti-war books?'
'No. What *do* you say, Harrison Starr?'
'I say, 'Why don't you write an anti-*glacier* book instead?'
Kurt Vonnegut, *Slaughterhouse Five*

All mountains were once seashores. See the gull fossils floating lazily among the updrafts, the warm air billowing from the raised dolerite that fences these ranges; see the sand whipped up with the westerly sleet, the rolling waves flecking up the highland tarns. And all sea-shores were once mountains. Note the scissored treeline, the rusting trig boats and the sinking dunes, the view blown forcefully into your face. Undulations in landscape – in time, not in space.

Mock their preference for settled vistas. They climb with seahorses.

Typical, these walkers, counting down hours in the public service for weekends hidden in boots and tents. The good gear crushed into their packs, not the latest – there are the kids' dentists and they're hoping to visit Vietnam next year. A trip into the central highlands, a chill mist in the morning scrubbed away by a clear day nodding to forecasts as they follow the dull lake track into the southern reserve; a few hours of moss and waterfalls, centuries of wilderness calendars, occasional breaks in the scrub edging the lake; flat water today, flat and deep. Across the narrow waist, the Traveller Range with Mt. Ida pointing skywards; she has noticed the sun, and even the high peaks are surprised at this bright warmth boiling from the east.

At Echo Point they stop for a bite and a drink. The jetty ramp sinking into the dense water, a path more certain, intractable. The massive old myrtle disguised as a snow gum, and the old hut, always half-built, the simple bunks and pot-belly stove, the sneaking smell of rats and the small beach so often covered with sun-bathed snow.

Sandwiches stowed in their stomachs, they lurch beneath their packs and tramp towards the lake's north face.

They'll try to climb Mt. Gould tomorrow, hoping the day will swell with weather to make the summit a gift worth revealing.[1] It's supposed to clag up in the morning, one of those days when the ice creeps between your layers, sending you angry and forlorn and hungry in your head. No views, just a heavy trudge through the thoughtless, slippery cloud, hoping the GPS batteries hold their charge as you retrace your track down the slippery steps collapsing under your feet. There are better days, there are memories.

But today, after stepping down from the junction with the track to Byron Gap, after stomping the hollow boards bridging the saturated plains, they open the stiff door of Narcissus Hut to a library of graffiti, a tangle of arguments and exclamation marks, a thicket of text, bauera blending with scoparia and cutting grass and tea-tree, too great a commotion to press on through, a mass signifying nothing to the walkers' shocked eyes as the woman scrawls another slogan on the calm walls.

They know her face instantly from the broadcasts, her thin figure patrolling the edge of Parliament House, certain and alone, strident in the cameras' grab. Railing, a forceful sentry. Pleading, urging all to consider the damage, the ripping and carving, the great white whales roaring and tearing, the ice blazing into the landscape. Ascribing guilt and judgement; yes, and though erosion fights on many fronts, there's the wind, the breath scouring its annual millimetres of layered stone, there's the water, infiltrating, freezing and flexing, there's the rivers burrowing open tunnels like wombats in the sun, but listen, she says, her weary grey ponytail leaning against her neck, her sign yelling

1 So far, a conventional walking story. Little local colour, no raconteur-ish, self-effacing flavour; wouldn't make *Tasmanian Tramp*. They're hoping to climb Gould? What of it? It's been climbed before.

beside her pernickety voice, as all around the faces whisper together, listen, she intones as a jaw in the flowing audience drops, laughs, the ice lady, the dumb fucking ice lady, listen, raising her arms, shouting, we must, *they* must absolutely be stopped.[2]

This is the lady met by our walkers,[3] stirring up arguments beside one of her alleged ancient battlefields. An apposite location, the scene of the crime. Murder-taping the borders of the national park, stitching up the slopes with cairns.

The walkers think to close the door and pivot on worn legs. They haven't signed up for this tour of deep agendas and when all

---

2 She's protesting what? *Glaciers?*

3 …with a few tokens of realism pinched from Pam Clarke. Don't know Pam Clarke? In the nineties, she was always on the news. An old lady protesting battery chicken farming: the chickens debeaked and sardined in cages built for mice, fed ghastly unknowns and blinded into constant egg-laying wakefulness. All alone she'd make a stand even as she was mocked and abused. I expect the chickens added to the theatre; she certainly danced with a two-metre tall hen named Battery Bertha on the steps of Parliament House. You can look it up: http://www.utas.edu.au/library/companion_to_tasmanian_history/C/Pam%20Clarke.htm One time I believe she locked herself in a tiny cage. Maybe she even apparelled herself in feathers. I'm not sure, no-one here has bothered with detailed research. *He's* just gathered a few notes to fill out the score, to make this anti-glacier woman, this neo-Pam, just a little less thin. The original would be loved these days; an archetype of before-her-time. All these foodies who have never held a real chicken while it wiggles its wings would be soldiering behind her, raising their placards. Picture them breaking into Ingham farms and setting the hens free as the executives run around in their moustaches and their flustered suits, scurrying in a wide shot, hopelessly trying to usher the chooks that leap from their hands towards the property gates while the protesters laugh, they laugh; we are watching this groundbreaking Australian film and we laugh and laugh, she's a good woman. She's an icon.

is said and done, they're not sympathetic; they love what the glaciers have accomplished and that's why they're stalking the shattered dolerite that tumbles around the central reserve. They are not wandering round the gentle fishing country on the east side; who would exchange this landscape made perfect in suffering for the slow, low hills that rise unpersuasively, mimicking the pastoral homelands suburbing the city? Is there something more human or more inhuman in broken, staggering rock? What space does the contrast between valley and peak provide, and which of these landscapes is cowering?

They're not planning on discussing any of this, but she has turned expectantly, she is waiting; will they say anything? Will she? If they turn now, nothing will have happened, nothing at all, and they could camp nearby, fetch water from the river – they were thinking about using the tent anyway – or given there's a couple of hours of daylight left, they could even push on to the plateau and get an early start in the morning before the weather goes to shit. Might bag up a few views after all; it would be nice to open up a sunset on top.

But in truth, they're just a little furious.

Not at the slogans, so much;[4] it's not about her message. It's that someone has the temerity to be writing on the walls of Narcissus Hut. If you can understand: in the parks, the huts are respected as much as the wildflowers, tarns and alpine scenery. They are common ground like no other place; not churches, libraries or cafes. Consolidating all the functions of shelter in a rough room. There are bridges and tracks, there are signs; all these are transitory. The huts gather and express our humanity around a glowing coal stove.

So while conventional walking etiquette is to keep your mouth sewn

---

4 Not even at the dubious allegories depicting climate change this writer seems to be blaring? Come on, stop hiding behind Pam, confess your grubby agenda. Do you rather like the idea of tearing up the ice and scattering it over the globe?

even when someone is pushing boundaries, a quiet fire on the sandy south west, a walking dog loosing its tongue around Ben Lomond – mention it in passing to a ranger back where the roads begin – there's something in this gratuitous urban behaviour that leads one of the walkers to open their mouth and ask: what are you doing?

And so they're committed. They take a few steps inside, drop their packs.

What are you doing, scrawling on the walls of Narcissus?

She invokes the silence a little longer as the walkers read the lines folding her cheeks and mouth and eyes, and then she begins, she makes her case from the whirlwind even as the sun sends stray visions into the dark hut. Have you seen the bullet holes, she asks, have you seen what the flows have done to the ground? Carving the cirques and moraines that follow their obese gait? There, she indicates to the south, St. Clair, the deepest lake in Australia. Know why? It wasn't flooded for Hydro power, I can tell you. The ice armies marching, advancing and wiping out the fresh-faced stones, plucking them from their families and slaving them downhill, roaring in a battle cry of cracking, twisting bones. Bulldozing the landscape before anybody dreamed of damming Pedder. Chiselling the valleys, deeper and deeper, bleeding the lakes into open wounds. Pouring blankness over the detailed green. Oh yes, she nods, the faces of the men clear and wary of believing, I know you find it all beautiful, sublime. You'll walk in peace and find yourselves refreshed. A bit stiff and sore afterwards; though it's not your knees that were drilled clean through. Be thankful they've retreated, sailed off to the south with their invasions. This is a destitute landscape you are walking in, this is a landscape weeping over its brokenness and scars.[5]

---

5   What exactly is he getting at? Oh I'm clear there's an *irony*; that wiping out the glaciers has actually become a realistic goal. Vonnegut's kooky analogy – its time has passed. Can't stop wars, can stop glaciers? That's the point?

It's not so long, but long enough. She stops, throws her marker to the ground and waits for a reaction from the walkers. There is little to say, she has washed across them like a strong southerly, and there is no answer to a southerly, you have to wait until it blows out. They treat her with such precedents in mind. One retrieves the marker and shoves it dutifully into the front of his pack as though it is a piece of rubbish mucking up a campsite.

Can see what you're saying, sure, says the other walker, nodding, consoling.[6] Just maybe don't write your stuff on the walls? Makes its own mess, you see. They are smiling gently, as though she has burst into tears on a long, scrubby climb, tentative, as though she is one of their unbalanced mothers. Yep, nods the walker with the marker locked firmly in his bag, that's right, but you've a right to what you're saying. And I've never looked at it that way before. He goes so far as to briefly broaden his smile.

She is watching them, more passionate than agitated, but slowly her flushed face pools. She walks across and picks up her daypack from the table.

Are you going out with the boat, mate? one walker asks. Shouldn't be too far off, we had a chat this morning at Cynthia Bay, they said there was a decent party coming up. Scout troop, I think.

What then? She has knocked on their door, missioned on their turf. She has said her piece, but they are clearly unpersuaded. They

6   Really? Because I'm still baffled by this text's *redundance*. The glaciers are disappearing anyway; why would anyone need to marshal spirits, advocate and argue for their end? As the glaciers dehydrate, slump over and perish – it's like lobbying for the night to fall. So then. Is the writer *against* climate change, but trying to be artful, less direct than Ian McEwan's *Solar*? That was a terrible book. Or is he melting away our time like so many fat, deceitful texts, grabbing at our minds and slowing us down?

will sleep tonight in the hut, they will boil life into their dehydrated food, sip their port, then sleep long on the flat wooden beds till the discomforts of morning bring them to life, assessing the day, their movements – cups of tea, pissing off the hut's deck. They will climb, if they can, into the old glacial heights, even as she follows the thawed furrow back to Cynthia Bay, the winding Lyell Highway escorting her to the Hobart coast, to her blogs and her petitions and her rallies, to her grinding, surplus campaign, while all around the landscape stretches, leans back in waves and sand, in mud and in scree, and remembers and forgets and remembers.[7]

7   A strange image I'm left with: an exhibition, photographs of Mawson's Antarctic huts, the ice pressing in on the door and filling up the rooms, old mugs, papers... and two books caught and frozen solid, unmoving and unread.

The Bridge

We're running out of time; paving the streets with our striding feet, packs pounding our hips, back and forth. A set of glaring traffic lights and the roar of fallen timber; a log truck gearing down the hill. Sacks of oats and potatoes sleeping on the footpaths. The drivers and their cigarettes, the smoke layering their singlets, rare fares welling with bustling locals; their aching elbows, assertive bags launched into back seats. Children, their small hands grasped like the shopping. There are no pedestrians, there are rivals, there are drivers and there are irises meeting over black asphalt. I am steadily ignoring the flowering wattlebirds, the bright greenhood orchids, thin and demure, poking from cracks in the concrete. Sweat glues my shoulders to my shirt. I wipe my arm across my forehead. 'Are we going to make it?' you ask with a voice that knocks gently before entering.

I carve a smile, check my phone and snare your neck with a stiff arm. 'We'll be right. We'll get a lift.'

Thumbing in the back teeth of the city where the roads flow east, tentative suggestions of parkland. 'A taxi,' you had suggested at the backpackers, 'I'm sure they could call us one, what do you think?' The young receptionist had leaned back at the counter, staring at a screen. I thought of nights long past when the last bus had roosted in its shed and my lone feet were stuck in the reeling city. The long, quiet walk beside the river, the headlights. The breeze of memories across the bridge – the ship that shattered its pylon shins, the sunken ship that lay sleeping in the depths of the river, beneath the rebuilt bridge; all that concrete so fragile under my feet. The esplanade spooning the bays, houses creeping from the water into ashen hills. One night, an easy-going woman with her old porch couch of a van, concertina curtains screening the rear, good-turning me out of her way to my father's dark house over the water. That house; windows full of river, southerly changes pouring clouds upstream and shaping them in waves.

'This is my town,' I had remarked, lightly proprietorial. 'We'll get a lift down the street for half their price.'

Money. We have been clipping tokens this week, sleeping on staircases and gathering our food from under tables, sparrowing expenses as I've tried to unearth memories. Much is different here, but I had imagined we would find that lady with her wide hair and rustic van, that we would borrow a ride to the new ferry over the river, that it would murmur us to the art parading on the north shore of Bruny, landscapes in the land, the piles of grey driftwood, quartzite, sex and life.

But the footpath is an uneven grid; the minutes give up and leave us, we waver left and right, a weary string section, and I wish that I had burnt a few dollars and taken your suggestion as my own; that I had argued just enough and then relented, patronised. *If it makes you feel better, fine.* You are travelling well, just behind me, and I am trying to find something to blame you for, to explain that next time, it would really be more helpful, when a dusty green van pulls over, more blurred than the one I remember, with windows open and bent roof-racks carrying a scavenged door. The driver with his grey hair and narrow face, his moustache patching wrinkles. His son, perhaps, with mainland hip-hop beating from his earphones, his blank sunglasses and labelled shirt. He speaks to me, the music still plugged into his head.

'You guys need a lift? We were thinking maybe you needed to hit the ferry. Not many taxis around yeah?'

'A lift?' I look down the road. 'Sure we need a lift.' My pack leans back, its harness straps me tightly, as though I'm dangling from a height.

'Cool,' he says out the passenger window. He looks back towards his father. 'Well, we can take you for maybe twenty bucks? What do you reckon?' This is pantomime. His father is smiling beatifically. A lift, yes, a lift.

'Twenty?' I shake my head. It's a driveway van, after all. This is all locals and under the counter. 'Look, we'd go for ten, but twenty's way too much for us.'

You are careful not to put your hand on my arm.

'Twenty,' he repeats, his father's head nodding beside his own. 'We're going like the total other direction. We have to come all the way back over here again.'

'C'mon, I'm from here,' I say, steady and sure. 'But thanks anyway.' It's time to walk away, the next step in the haggling process. They'll be expecting this. What's more, just a little further down Macquarie Street a real, solid gold taxi is emptying its tin of baked passengers. I run awkwardly with the bouncing pack; you are chasing somewhere behind me as I reach the window. The slumped, bored driver: 'Ferry port? You'll take us to the ferry port?'

He agrees blearily. We reach towards the back doors. 'How much?' I remember to ask. 'It's a flat rate, ten dollars, isn't it?' And perhaps he is about to acquiesce, perhaps we are about to open our doors and sling our gear securely on top of our laps, perhaps we are about to pour down the road, past the old regatta grounds, the tugboats and the mild river, over the bridge connecting with our ferry; perhaps the tension has loosened and all we need to do is stare, confident, concerned, at the calculations of the digital clock as they flicker towards three in the afternoon. But the young man from the van is gesturing, roughly, at the driver's window.

'This is our guy, he's riding with us, if you take him anywhere we will seriously...' and the driver shrugs, revs a few metres on and searches the narrow crowd for a free, unencumbered passenger.

'That's it,' I say, raising my palms and throwing them down towards the ground. 'No, thanks. No way.' I drag you down the road, beyond the horizon of the young man's protests, his yelling. We will find a real taxi or we will return shamefaced to the backpackers or we will walk, we will trudge along the domain highway, weighed down by our clothes and our Huon bowls and the water freshly gathered from the mountain rivulets. Our feet dissolving in our boots. We will camp hard on the concrete bicycle path flanking the bridge, we will scavenge among the railings on the empty night tarmac, we will catch the boat next morning, stay for one, two days and miss our flight in a puddle of righteous frustration.

When you wipe your hand gently through my hair, saying, 'Look, we really need to get a ride,' I turn to face you properly for the first time in nearly half an hour. I remember your ears and your cheeks and your nose, the load slumping your back, I remember that you have been calm and considerate and that even as I hunt for ways to disperse my rage, it is being channelled down a highway at the end of which I imagine you sitting, vague and judgmental. And I am sorry, for a moment I am sorry. And as the van catches us again, crumbling and full of scars, I remember that it is faster than our staggering steps.

The old man has put on a hat and the young man has taken off his sunglasses; a fresh start, a new beginning. 'You need to go to the ferry port?'

'How much?' I ask again, reluctant but prepared to grasp necessity. 'How much?'

'Ten dollars,' they say, 'we'll take you there for ten dollars.' They are almost kneeling in their seats. The van is chipped and old. We climb into the back seat and rest our backpacks on our knees as though we are at a circus and they are our children, slumped on the shapes cast by our tired legs. The van pulls out into traffic, we are on our way, I take hold of your hand and bend your watch towards me. It is still only a quarter to three, we should be fine, we are going to just make it.

We are moving. There is time and space, now, to worry about other things. As we burn past the cenotaph, the Baha'i centre and the old Regatta pavilion, I become aware that we are in a grubby van, with two men who have no endorsement, no card identifying them, no photo hanging from the rear-view and mirroring their faces. Where could they be taking us? We have heard stories, read warnings on lurid, earnest websites. The back of an old sewerage works, our laptop and our cash. An ATM and a firm, polite knife. As we leave the city and roll past the Domain, flat-hilled and speckled with sandstone centres, the empty green pastures, gardens of grass and oak, we check and make sure, we are constantly staring and notating out the window, we are touring omens. You fiddle with the name-tag buckled to your pack, look at it and read it.

I pull a sharp pen from my pocket and hold it in my hand.

To our right, the river is a deep blue-grey. Over on the far bank are yachts clustered in bays; the road curtails the view of our own side, the slippery blocks of mudstone, but we can see the old railway line lying wistfully, hoping for exercise. The windows of the van are broad and open. As the driver indicates for the bridge, the salty humidity eases our fears. We turn to each other and smile.

Your eyes flick forwards.

The father is reaching back, he is trying to hand over a scrappy notebook and a pen. 'Write your name, your address here.'

'What?' I ask, 'what do you mean?' But I take the bunched stationery, find myself with two pens, slip one back into my pocket.

'Write down your name and address,' he repeats as I shuffle through the pages, reading other names, travellers from Devonport, Stanley, Coles Bay, and I see that this is his identification, his reference, his testimonial, and then all at once I am master of the present. We are safe and we will make the boat, we are safe, he is begging for my endorsement and I will oblige, I will help the poor bloke out. I begin to write my details, but a wary creativity takes over, sabotaging my surname and sending my phone number into a sequence of digits, primes perhaps, or a Fibonacci progression, posting a toy address, an invented avenue off the island, in the suburbs of Whitemark. The driver's eyes alternate between the front and back, the bridge and the image of us securely scribbling.

His son's glasses, poised above his head, spill towards the dashboard. He may have shouted, or pointed ahead. There is skidding, a lurch.

~

Perhaps it had been building over the decades, strange blends of moon and rain, the gale force tides and the river's meandering press, and all it took was a droplet to dislodge the broken ship from the muddy bottom.

Tossing and turning on her restless riverbed; the elements, this time, piloted the ship sideways like an axe into the quivering pylons, a submarine attack that toppled the centre spans, sinking the bridge to its knees in a second storm of concrete and steel.

The view up and down river. A few seagulls resting on the railings. In the distance, framed by our windscreen, a car leaps cinematically.

We all wait silent; our words could overbalance the scales. We are a photograph repeated, folklore made terrifying flesh. We are in books, yellowed newspaper articles, the museum display with the glass and the plasticine wreck. We are waiting to fall as others fell, we are waiting to die; we are waiting to live as others did, going on to tell the story for years, waking from dreams with our feet landing on our mattresses after stamping at the empty, groundless air.

Are we on time, I think, are we still on time?

Tiny bird movements from the men, easing their weight towards the rear. The father points silently at the van's back door. You reach slowly, so slowly, to slide the door back, to open the way for us to tiptoe quietly, urgently to the safety of the cliff's edge, to feel the fresh vertigo of what might have been, of what might still be. As you rest one foot on the bitumen I gently manoeuvre my pack behind me, counterweighting the vehicle, and get ready to escape. The son kneels in the cavern between the front seats. I hear a moist rustle and become aware of the pages in my hand.

I look up to meet your gaze, then reach into my pocket for the other pen. In a trembling scrawl, I complete the fake address in the notebook. I barely lean across to hand it to the old man waiting in the doorway.

He looks down, takes it in his fingers and nods.

Acknowledgements

In the first instance, I'm grateful to friends and family who have read and improved these stories over the years – Michael Blake, Anneliese Milk, Emily Thomson, and particularly Robbie Arnott and Adam Ouston, for their patient suggestions, friendship and commiserations over a particularly long haul. Without their efforts, these stories would be so much worse.

I'm also tremendously grateful to all the literary journals who have found a home for these pieces, and the editors who have supported my work – especially Rachel Edwards, Jennifer Mills and Jonathan Green. Earlier versions of these stories first appeared in a number of Australian journals: 'The Economist', 'We Are All Superman', 'It's All Happening Here', 'All Hollows' and 'What Fear Was' in *Overland;* 'Atlantis Minor' and 'Flathead Out One Day' in *Meanjin;* 'An Anti-Glacier Book', 'Beast Evolving' and 'Landscape within Landscapes' in *Island;* 'The Lake' in *Kill Your Darlings;* 'The Bridge' in *Griffith Review;* 'The Slide' in *The Big Issue;* 'A Visitor's Guide to the Huts of Mt Wellington: 1913' in *The Lifted Brow;* and 'The Eradication Program' in *The Review of Australian Fiction.* 'Below Tree Level' first appeared as a short book and artistic installation developed with Leigh Rigozzi and supported by The Australia Council, and 'Conglomerate' was first published in 2017 as a fictiõnella for *Lost Rocks* (2017–21), a slow-publishing artwork by Justy Phillips & Margaret Woodward / A Published Event, Hobart. These journals and publishers provide a crucial space for literature in this country, and I'll always be appreciative of the opportunities they have made for my writing.

I'm grateful to all of those people who have provided encouragement and support at important times, when it was difficult to see a way forward: Pete Hay, Anne Kellas, Richard Flanagan, Peter Timms, Danielle Wood, Richard Wastell, Susie Greenhill, Jane Rawson, Ralph Wessman and the superb Tasmanian literary, bookselling and walking communities.

My sincere appreciation to Troy Ruffels and the Bett Gallery for permission to use the fabulous image on the jacket, and to Ryan O'Neill, Jennifer Mills and Robbie Arnott for their kind words.

Tremendous thanks to my agent, Martin Shaw, and publisher, Ed Wright. Without your efforts and encouragement, there would be no book.

Finally, love and thanks to my parents for their long-term support, and my family – Rachel, Augie, Daisy and Rui – for being a home for me.